A dedicated reader and scribbler all her life, ROSIE JAMES completed her first novel (sadly unpublished) before reaching her teens.

Significant success came much later, and over the last twelve years newspaper and magazine articles, short stories and romantic novels followed under her other pen name Susanne James.

Rosie's four family sagas were the next stage, the plots reflecting her fascination with the human condition – how different, yet how alike we all are. And in every story one thing is guaranteed – a happy ending.

Also by Rosie James

Letters to Alice
The Long Road Ahead
Lexi's War

Front Line Nurse

ROSIE JAMES

ONE PLACE. MANY STORIES

HQ
An imprint of HarperCollins*Publishers* Ltd
1 London Bridge Street
London SE1 9GF

First published in Great Britain by
HQ, an imprint of HarperCollins*Publishers* Ltd 2019

Copyright © Rosie James 2019

Rosie James asserts the moral right to be
identified as the author of this work.
A catalogue record for this book is
available from the British Library.

ISBN: 9781848457928

MIX
Paper from
responsible sources
FSC
www.fsc.org **FSC® C007454**

This book is produced from independently certified FSC™ paper
to ensure responsible forest management.

For more information visit: www.harpercollins.co.uk/green

Printed and bound in Great Britain by
CPI Group (UK) Ltd, Croydon CR0 4YY

For my ever-loving family...
Including our precious dogs.

Chapter 1

November 1900

Randolph Garfield stood on the quayside and watched the last huge roll of tobacco being wheeled into his main warehouse. He nodded, satisfied at the superb quality of this consignment, but what had he expected? Virginian tobacco was the finest in the world.

As usual, his trusted foreman was checking each roll as it was stored away safely, and Randolph glanced at his watch. It was late and all the other workers had already gone home. But they would be back here again tomorrow morning, seven o'clock sharp.

Observing the proceedings closely, as he always did, Randolph tightened his hand on his walking cane. He liked the feel of its smooth, round marble head beneath his palm – palpable even through the fine kid gloves he was wearing – and considered the cane as something of a talisman, because it had belonged to his father who had never left the house without it.

Garfield Tobacco, its name marked out in huge steel lettering across the entrance of the three warehouses, was well known in the East End as it had been for two generations before Randolph. His father had died very young, which meant that Randolph had

had to accept leadership of the family firm earlier than he might have expected. But he was not resentful in any way. He had been born into prosperity and enjoyed the life of the prosperous, and was giving 3-year-old Alexander, his only son and heir, the same privileges. So it was highly likely that Alexander, too, would follow in the family footsteps when Randolph no longer wished to head the business. He shrugged briefly. There was plenty of time to worry about that because, after all, he was only 40.

When the warehouse was fully secure, Randolph began to make his way from the docks envisaging how those gigantic rolls of tobacco would soon be transformed into thousands of cigarettes, cigars, plug and pipe tobacco and snuff, all supplying the never-ending needs of the public, rich or poor. The pleasure and solace of smoking was a gift of the gods. Certainly a gift for Garfield's.

It was a miserable, late November evening, the gloom only slightly lessened by pale overhead lighting. Randolph took his usual route from the docks along the cobbled streets, past rows and rows of ramshackle, terraced houses and countless pubs. He had long since become accustomed to the poverty and depriva-tion all around, the overpowering scent of unwashed bodies and human excrement, of coal smoke hanging permanently in the air, the persistent smell of beer. There were always groups of children hanging about outside, few wearing any shoes, and who never seemed to go to bed, whatever time it was. Randolph doubted any of them had ever seen the inside of a classroom, despite the Education Act three decades earlier having decreed that education should be compulsory.

Throughout the area, various sorts of trading seemed to go on… there were countless private beer and cider houses, and women offering rags and old pots and pans for sale. A prolific number of people were engaged in the dangerous process of match-making, while little 'match girls' stood on every corner hoping to sell for a few pennies, and very young children persis-tently offered themselves to anyone willing to pay for it. Once,

2

Randolph had been approached by a small girl, no more than seven or eight years old, earnestly offering him a 'good time'. He had been appalled and had brushed her away, but the incident had haunted him for a long time afterwards.

But there was no doubt that the economy was booming, all the workshops and factories along the docks were doing well – including that of his great friend, Jacob Mason, whose business was in steel, and the manufacture of nuts, bolts and allied merchandise. Randolph walked on with a lighter step. It was a wonderful feeling to be successful at what you did. He and Jacob spent many happy hours discussing current topics and airing their opinions about the government. The two men had attended many meetings together but Randolph admitted that he did not always agree with his friend. Jacob had very strong views, and was always convinced he was right.

Now, Randolph began to reach quieter streets where the air was slightly cleaner, and he would soon get to the point at which he would normally hail a carriage to take him home to the house in which he'd been born – an elegant, three-storey dwelling in leafy Belsize Park. It was perfectly situated, and sometimes Randolph would take the long walk from Primrose Hill to Parliament Hill where he could be alone with his thoughts. And Hampstead Heath and Regent's Park were close by, lovely open spaces for children to run and play. Randolph himself had done so and Alexander, too, sometimes went there with his nanny.

Randolph's eyes clouded briefly. He could give his son everything that money could buy but he could not give him back his mother who had died giving birth to their only baby. They had planned to have many more children but it was not to be. Sybil had been 30 years old when she'd eventually conceived, and the love of Randolph's life. And although he was considered an attractive man, being tall and broad-shouldered with scarcely any grey hair, he knew he would never marry again. Alexander's mother could never be replaced.

Trying to shake off the occasional bout of depression he suffered from, Randolph walked on more quickly. If he hurried, he might be in time to wish Alexander goodnight before the little boy fell asleep.

Suddenly, as he rounded one of the many corners of this lightly populated area Randolph's progress was instantly halted, and he frowned. What had he almost tripped over just then? Something or other had been tucked to one side, but was certainly an obstruction to anyone walking by. He narrowed his eyes and crouched down, his expression changing to one of genuine horror as he realised what he was looking at.

He found himself gazing down into the small face of a very young baby whose large brown eyes were pooled in the purest white.

Still crouching, Randolph took a deep breath. This tiny infant had clearly been abandoned, in a cardboard box like rubbish. How could anyone do such a thing? Yet he could see that the baby was warmly wrapped in a huge, pale grey knitted shawl and soft white bonnet, and under the chin had been tucked a small pink teddy bear. Someone had loved this child…

Very carefully, Randolph picked up the box, and was surprised by its light weight. He held it to him protectively as he stood up and looked around. The street was quiet and deserted, with no sign of whoever may have left the child there, but luckily Randolph knew that no more than two hundred yards away there was the orphanage. It had been there for years, and he breathed a sigh of relief. They would take the child.

He walked very slowly towards the huge grey building, not wanting to disturb the baby, who had not made a single sound but was just lying there looking up at him. Randolph gritted his teeth. How could anyone leave this beautiful baby?

Randolph could not have been aware of the fragile young girl watching him from her hiding place, nor have heard the rustle of her thin skirt as she crept back into the shadows.

4

Reaching the orphanage, he rang the bell and waited, and after a few moments he heard approaching footsteps marching across a stone floor. Then, heavy bolts were moved aside and the door opened. A tall, angular woman stood there, unsmiling.

'Yes? What is it?' Then, on seeing a distinguished looking man there and not another vagrant begging for food, the woman moved to one side. 'Oh... would you like to come in?'

Randolph accepted the invitation and carefully handed over the baby.

'I found this a few moments ago,' he said quietly, 'down there at the far end of the road.' He paused. 'I am sure you will know what to do about it.'

The woman looked down at the box and tutted. 'Oh not another little throw-out,' she said abruptly. 'It's a pity these sluts of girls don't think before they—'

'Quite,' Randolph said quickly.

Together they moved inside and the woman placed the box on a large oak table. And there in the pale lighting they could make out the neat printing on the side.

Angelina. Born 1st November 1900. Weight 6 lb. 3 ozs.

'This little bastard's only three weeks old, and tiny,' the woman said. 'It could have caught its death out there like that. Good job you came by when you did, sir.'

Just then, another woman approached and took in the familiar situation at a glance. 'Oh dear,' she said, her voice soft. She looked up at Randolph. 'I am Emma Kingston, the superintendent here.'

She was a short, stout lady, her thick grey hair piled up into a knot, her face dominated by thoughtful blue eyes. Randolph smiled briefly.

'I am sorry to disturb you, Miss Kingston,' he said. 'My name is Randolph Garfield and I found this child less than an hour ago. The box had been placed to one side of the pavement.' He cleared his throat. 'I am sure you will know how to deal with this... unfortunate matter.'

5

Emma Kingston glanced at the other woman. 'Thank you, Mrs Marshall,' she said, and with that, Mrs Marshall departed without a backward glance.

After she had gone, Miss Kingston studied the printing on the box, then picked up the baby and tenderly held it to her. She sighed. 'I am afraid we do get children handed in here from time to time,' she said, 'but not usually this young, and not usually in a box.'

For the first time, the baby made a small pathetic gurgle – which made Randolph catch his breath. Why had this happened to him? And after such a long day!

After a moment, Miss Kingston said, somewhat apologetically, 'Would you mind following me into my office for a few seconds, Mr Garfield? It is always useful to have something definitive to add to my records. Purely a formality,' she added, 'but you never know, someone may eventually come forward and claim Angelina... this little angel.'

Randolph followed the superintendent along the hallway and into the living quarters. There seemed to be a lot of doors, all closed, and despite this being an orphanage there was little sound. But of course, it was now getting very late.

In Miss Kingston's office, Randolph took the chair he was offered and sat down. After putting the box with the baby in it down on a chair beside her, Miss Kingston took out a ledger and opened a fresh page. She looked across at Randolph.

'I take it you are Mr Garfield of Garfield Tobacco?' she enquired politely, and Randolph nodded.

'Indeed I am,' he said quietly.

'So, Mr Garfield, would you tell me exactly when and where you found this baby" Miss Kingston said, and for the next two minutes Randolph told her the little there was to say.

Presently, Miss Kingston sat back, looking pensive. 'It's fortunate that we are still here,' she said, 'because the orphanage will be closing at the beginning of next year.'

Randolph was surprised. The place had always been here. He frowned. 'So – what will happen to all the children?' he asked. 'Where will they go?'

The superintendent turned to take the baby in her arms again, rocking it to and fro comfortingly, and Randolph realised that the lady clearly loved children and must have looked after so many in her time. Unlike the other woman who had seemed cold and unfeeling.

'Fortunately, we only have eight orphans with us at the moment,' Miss Kingston said. 'I have tried to cut back because of the impending closure, but normally there are fifteen children here. The ones remaining will be dispersed to other orphanages when we can find places for them. It can be anywhere in the country, of course,' she added. 'Not necessarily local.'

Randolph was feeling more unhappy with every moment that passed. Little children, little babies like Angelina, being passed around like parcels. He cleared his throat.

'But why is the orphanage to close?'

'Lack of funding, I'm afraid,' the superintendent said. 'Of course, we get a little parish relief but our principal benefactor died earlier this year, and sadly he left no provision for the orphanage in his will.' She paused, smiling briefly. 'He had been more than generous in his lifetime and I don't think there was very much left in the end.'

Randolph looked away for a second. 'And what will you do, Miss Kingston? Will you accompany any of the children who have been in your care?'

Miss Kingston shook her head sadly. 'I think it is time for me to finish what has been my life's work,' she said, 'though I had had every intention of remaining here for perhaps another ten years when I retire. But fate has taken a hand, so when the orphanage closes, that will be my own farewell, too.'

*

7

Randolph left the orphanage and walked on slowly. It was strange, but he had never given that place much thought at all – or rather, had never given those children much thought. They were safe and provided for, and much like the youngsters down by the docks, orphans were merely a fact of life. There had always been orphans and there would always be orphans. So why was he, Randolph Garfield, feeling uneasy?

Well, he knew the reason. That little child, that tiny baby, Angelina, had caused him to stop and do something to help her. Those beautiful eyes looking at him like that had secured a place in his conscience.

And in his heart…

The following evening, Jacob Mason came to Number 1 Richmond Villas to enjoy a bottle of good red wine with his friend. This was a ritual which had taken place every other week for years, and the wine was always accompanied by a light supper of cold meats and pickles and a loaf of bread baked and served by Randolph's housekeeper.

But the main purpose of these occasions was to talk shop, to discuss current events and the state of the world in general. And then they'd exchange news of more personal matters. Tonight, Randolph did have something to recount.

As the two sat either side of a bright log fire in his study, Randolph spoke up. 'On my way home yesterday evening, Jacob, I had a most uncomfortable experience.'

Jacob sat forward, immediately interested. 'Go on.'

'I found… I happened upon… well, I discovered a newborn baby which had been abandoned in a cardboard box. And it was a complete shock, I can assure you"

Jacob nodded, but seemed unsurprised at the news. 'What did you do about it?'

'I took the box to the orphanage just up the road from where I found it – and on the side of the box were the words – "Angelina, born 1st November 1900 weight 6 lbs. 3oz".'

'Oh well, that's all right then,' Jacob said casually 'It'll be fed and clothed and looked after until it can get out into the world and fend for itself.' He sat back, satisfied with his own summing up of the sad facts.

Not for the first time in his life, Randolph felt angry at his friend's attitude. To hear Jacob refer to that innocent child as an 'it' was upsetting. He let a moment pass, then said, 'I was very surprised to learn that the orphanage is to close in the New Year. Due to a lack of funding, apparently.'

'Well, money is what makes the world go around, as we all know,' Jacob said cheerfully. 'Other orphanages will take those kids I suppose.' He took a drink from his glass. 'Trouble is, Randolph, they can never *be* anything, amount to anything, give anything *back*,' Jacob went on. 'Just imagine the parentage! The genetic influence! I believe that orphans are usually illegitimate – bastards, in other words. So, genetically speaking, their prospects are hopeless. Hopeless!'

'I think that is a rather pessimistic view, Jacob,' Randolph said coolly. 'It's obvious that not everyone has the same start in life, but those children are schooled in arithmetic, they are given books to read, and they are taught the bible—'

Jacob interrupted, smiling. 'I can see that your recent experience has played on your mind and given you cause for thought, Randolph.'

Randolph nodded. 'I learned that nuns from the priory teach the children and help to look after them,' he said, 'together with a small, subsidiary domestic staff.'

Jacob shrugged. 'I'm telling you, none of them will ever amount to anything. They are the driftwood of life! My father was emphatic about never employing such people. because they'd always be a waste of time. And my father was never wrong about anything! All successful countries, all successful economies, depend on people of good stock, of good background, of intellect, and you and I are part of that, Randolph. We are doing our bit to keep the system going.' He leaned forward and tapped Randolph on the knee. 'And, in years to come, when our two youngsters tie the knot – oh, I know it won't be for a very long time yet – but when they do, they will be continuing the process. And they will produce children of distinction! Useful citizens, Randolph!'

Randolph smiled briefly. Who knew what Alexander might want to do with his life, or who he'd share that life with? Jacob's daughter, Honora, was still only an infant, but he and his wife Elizabeth, were determined that their little girl would one day be the next Mrs Garfield.

Randolph stared into his glass for a moment. He knew that Jacob was a great admirer of Frances Galton, the distinguished statistician and mathematician. Galton was of the opinion – among other things – that it was simple to place the populace in groups, from the lowest to the highest in terms of what they would be worth to the success of a country, and that the value of an 'average' person over a lifetime would be no more than five pounds. He also empathically believed that the lower classes should be discouraged from procreating.

'I returned to the orphanage today and spoke at length to the superintendent,' Randolph said, 'and I learned that there are two trustees, one of whom is a priest – Laurence Dunn—'

'Oh, I've met Father Laurence,' Jacob interjected. 'He's been to my club once or twice.'

'Anyway, I wanted to know if anyone had returned to claim little Angelina,' Randolph said, and Jacob snorted derisively.

'That'll never happen!' he said. 'Orphans are the unwanted in life. Certainly unwanted by the loose, ignorant women who spawn them!'

Chapter 2

The following Saturday afternoon, Randolph left the factory earlier than usual and made his way to the orphanage. He had been thinking long and hard about many things, and had come to a decision. He was not going to see the place close, its young inmates dispersed to heaven knew where. If it was at all possible, he would buy it – he'd already re-named it in his head. It would become the Garfield Home for Children.

His ring on the bell was answered almost at once by Mrs Marshall. She stood aside for Randolph to enter.

'Is it possible for me to speak to Miss Kingston?' he said briefly. 'I will not keep her long.'

Mrs Marshall nodded. 'I'll tell her,

Presently, sitting opposite Emma Kingston in her office, Randolph said – Firstly, I would like to find out how the baby... how Angelina is getting on. Is she thriving?'

The superintendent smiled. 'That little one is a born survivor, Mr Garfield,' she said. 'We engage a wet nurse for babies this young and Angelina took what was offered straightaway. She sleeps well, is no trouble at all and is so *alert*! In fact, I would say she is already looking around and sizing up the world she's been born into!'

Randolph nodded. Would he ever forget those large brown eyes gazing up at him?

'You say there are eight children here. Both girls and boys, I take it?'

'Yes, of course,' Emma Kingston said, 'At the moment we have four boys and, with Angelina now, there are five little girls..

nd how long do they remain at the orphanage? Generally speaking?'

'Normally until they are fourteen,' the superintendent said, 'Then we try and find work for them, and somewhere to live.' She shrugged briefly. 'It isn't easy, but sometimes a job comes up in one of the big houses or hotels, where they have bed and board in exchange for cleaning work, scullery work, or in the kitchen. And luckily, they do have some experience because from quite a young age they must help here with everyday tasks. It's never too early to learn such things, is it?' She smiled. 'The boys are not so keen, but they are kept busy in our small garden, weeding, clearing up and planting. We try to grow our own vegetables to keep our costs down,' she added.

Randolph cleared his throat. Why had he never given a thought to the small lives being lived out in this huge building, and other buildings like it?

'And what about staff, Miss Kingston?' he asked. 'How many people do you have working for you?'

'Oh well... I have Mrs Marshall, who you've met,' the superintendent replied. 'She is a general assistant and she comes in each day. One or two extra helpers are engaged occasionally when needed, and of course there are always the two domestics who clean and do regular hours in the laundry.'

'You have quite a task force here, Miss Kingston,' Randolph said, and she smiled.

'Ah, but I haven't mentioned our wonderful cook, Mrs Vera Haines! She is resident, naturally, as is our young nurse, Nancy' the superintendent said. 'Nancy is a cheerful young lady who sometimes helps the nuns in the schoolroom, or accompanies the children when they go to the park. But she goes home at weekends, so it's fortunate that, after all these years, I am well able to cope with any minor medical problems which may crop up. And of course, I can always call the parish doctor if necessary,' she added.

Randolph glanced at the clock on the wall. He didn't want to take up too much of the woman's time, but if he was going to put his plan into action, he had to know what he was taking on – and what it was going to cost. 'Would you mind showing me around, Miss Kingston?' he asked politely. 'Because I would very much like to help in some way if possible, and...'

Emma Kingston stood up. 'Of course you may look around, Mr Garfield,' she said, 'but I am afraid we are beyond help now. We just cannot afford to stay here with the small financial help we receive. The whole place is in need of a thorough overhaul, such lighting as we have needs replacing and the plumbing is in a poor state.' She shook her head sadly. 'So one has to face facts – this building is not fit for purpose, and that is why it is to be sold. Apart from the fact that, as I explained, our benefactor has died,' she added.

Randolph did not reply, but followed her along the corridor and up to the stairs to be shown the five small bedrooms for the orphans – all very neat and tidy, he noted to himself.

'These rooms at the end are the ones for Nancy, Mrs Haines and myself,' Miss Kingston said, 'and our nursery for the babies is there as well. The two small bathrooms we have are downstairs – which can be slightly inconvenient.'

Is Angelina in the nursery?' Randolph asked casually, and Emma Kingston stopped.

'Yes – would you like to take a peep, Mr Garfield?'

'Together, they went into the nursery and as Randolph gazed down at the child he had the greatest difficulty in not scooping her up into his arms. Cocooned in snow-white covers, she was fast asleep. On the soft white pillow was the pink teddy bear, the one tiny possession she had brought with her.

'She is the most delightful baby,' Miss Kingston murmured softly. 'We are all in love with her. It's as if she's determined to be no trouble to anyone.'

Just then, Angelina stirred and opened her eyes, and Randolph felt tears welling up in his own. What possible future was in store for this little one, abandoned at birth? Why couldn't she be his, his and Sybil's? One of the children they'd planned to have?

The superintendent interrupted his thoughts as she said quietly, 'Her next feed is almost due, but see? Angelina is looking at us, Mr Garfield, giving us the onceover! This is quite unusual in so young a child,' she added.

Randolph found his voice. 'She is... perfect,' he said. 'Surely a gift from God.'

Miss Kingston glanced at him covertly. For a hard-nosed businessman, Mr Garfield was rather a surprise.

'It is very quiet everywhere,' Randolph said as he followed her back down, and she half-turned to glance at him.

'Ah well, at this time on a Saturday afternoon the children are usually taken to the park – if the weather is reasonable – but they'll be back soon and looking forward to teatime. Cook usually makes cakes on Saturdays.'

Emma Kingston opened a door and gestured for Randolph to look inside. 'This is where food is eaten,' she said, 'and the children have three meals a day, breakfast, dinner and tea, and a warm drink last thing.'

Randolph looked down at the two long trestle tables, the wooden benches pushed beneath. 'I must say that I was aware of a very appetising smell as I came in earlier,' he said. 'So what was on the menu for dinner today?'

'It was tripe and onions today, with mashed potatoes, and an apple for pudding,' Miss Kingston said, 'and while tripe may not be everyone's first choice we are on a very tight budget, so the children must eat what they are given.' She smiled briefly. 'Orphans are not allowed to be fussy, Mr Garfield, but our cook always manages to make everything so tasty that it is unusual for even a scrap of food to be left on the plates. And the staff eat exactly the same.'

Finally, Randolph was shown the playroom and the schoolroom next to it, with the single desks in rows and a large blackboard and easel at the front of the class.

'Do the children enjoy their lessons with the nuns?' Randolph enquired. 'I mean, do you have behavioural problems?'

'Sometimes,' Miss Kingston admitted, 'but orphans are just children, all with difficult backgrounds – well, those we know about. But some of them are just picked up from the street, little strays that no one knows a thing about. So of course they can be naughty, but that's only to be expected– and I try and talk them out of their bad humour with a hug, and maybe a sweet or two,' she added.

Following her back into her office, Randolph decided that it was time to come clean.

'Miss Kingston,' he said, 'I have something to say which may come as a surprise, but all things being equal, I am going to buy this building, and will expect it to be run exactly as it is at the moment.'

The woman's reaction was immediate. 'Mr Garfield... Mr Garfield, I am not sure what to say, but—'

'The only thing I would ask you to say, Miss Kingston,' Randolph interrupted, 'is that, if it all goes through as I hope it will, would you stay on in your present position here and help me... advise me? My business life is obviously totally different from owning an orphanage, as you will appreciate, and I am going to need expert guidance. Can I dare to hope that you will provide that guidance?'

For a full ten seconds Emma Kingston didn't utter a word. Then she said simply, 'It would be my privilege, Mr Garfield. And my utter joy.'

He stood up to leave, then hesitated. 'It is very sad that no one has come forward to claim Angelina,' he said, and the superintendent nodded.

'Indeed it is,' she said quietly. 'And… I do have news which it grieves me to tell you, Mr Garfield. But the body of a young woman was found late on Thursday night, about half a mile from here and… it seems that she had quite recently given birth.'

Randolph felt his stomach lurch in horror at this information, yet he was well aware that almost every week in the year it was commonplace for nameless bodies to be swept up on the streets of London. Jacob Mason's classless, rootless, useless human beings…

Chapter 3

December 1913

Alone at home in his study, Randolph stared out at the cheerless wintry scene, his heart heavy with dread. There was no denying any longer that war with Germany was imminent. The newspapers were full of gloom – Mr Winston Churchill who, in the last couple of years, had demanded the construction of huge battleships to counter Germany's massive fleet, appeared to be hungry for the conflict to begin as soon as possible. And it seemed that he might get his wish because military exercises could be regularly witnessed on the streets of London and artillery batteries had appeared at the mouth of the Thames. Ready and waiting... Randolph ran a hand through his hair. The thought of war was hideous for many reasons – not only because of the blood, sweat and tears which would be shed, but the damage to the economy would be enormous, the wealth of the country eroded. Any seafaring trades would be affected, and that included Garfield's.

But all those considerations were not what was really making Randolph's stomach churn with anxiety. It was the fact that Alexander would almost certainly be the age at which he would be expected to join the British army and do his bit to help defend France and Belgium against the enemy. Randolph had kept a close watch on the news over the preceding months and had a shrewd idea as to what that would entail. The thought that his beloved son should come to harm, or suffer an early death, was the worst possible nightmare. If that did happen, Randolph himself would not wish to go on living.

He tried to cheer up. After all, in a couple of days Alexander would be coming home from his boarding school for the Christmas holidays, and despite everything, that was enough to ease Randolph's frown.

Ever since Alexander and Jacob Mason's daughter, Honora, had been born, the two families always spent the two main Christmas days together. The Masons had no other children, nor close family members, so it seemed a natural thing to do. The two families took it in turns to host the festivities and this year it was going to be at the Masons' house. Although, as usual, there would be merely five of them enjoying the festivities the noise and hilarity was always enough for a crowd. From very early days, the two children had always loved being together, and even now that they were both almost 17 years old, nothing had changed. As Jacob kept insisting, they had been a pigeon pair since birth, and he would always make sure that the ubiquitous sprig of mistletoe was there above the front door so that Honora and Alexander could be witnessed showing their special love for each other and receive a round of applause from Jacob and Elizabeth. But Randolph would merely smile. He hoped his friends were not going to be disappointed in their matchmaking hopes. Alexander seemed engrossed in his college life, and although, next year, he was expected to start a business degree course, Randolph had been advised that they should think again as his son showed an exceptional understanding of physics. It appeared that a different future might await him.

*

18

For Randolph, Christmas Eve was the occasion he most looked forward to. Ever since he had a acquired the orphanage, he had made a point of visiting the place several times every month, and Christmas Eve was a special date. He and Alexander would go there together and take presents and treats for the staff. Of course, the children always had a bulging stocking to open on Christmas morning, but it was the magic of the day before which touched Randolph the most. To hear his little orphans sing carols to him, and see their faces alive with hope and excitement, always pulled at his heart strings.

Now, glancing at his watch, he saw that it was almost time for his supper to be served, but first, he needed to look through some papers. Opening one of the drawers in his desk, a small brown envelope took his attention. Of course, he knew what it held because he had looked through it many times.

It was a bundle of precious letters that Miss Kingston had sent him some years ago. Letters that Randolph guarded with the same care that he gave to his important financial papers, because every child who had been capable of doing so had written to him telling him what they would like to be when they grew up and left the orphanage.

This exercise had been Miss Kingston's idea, and she could not have known the pleasure it would give to their benefactor every time he read the careful writing. There were going to be train drivers and policemen, writers and singers – one 8-year-old wanted to be the Archbishop of Canterbury, and several wanted to own their own sweet shops. But the thing was, they all had hopes, and Randolph did his best to help as many of them as he could. After all, he was influential and had already seen several of the 14-year-olds find work, giving them the chance to earn money and develop some self-respect and independence. Last year he had been especially pleased to see one of his youngsters, who'd always been top of the class in arithmetic, secure an apprenticeship with a firm of accountants – business associates of Randolph's.

And despite Jacob Mason's cynical outlook on orphans, over the last year or two he had agreed to take on three lads to work in his factory and had grudgingly admitted that, so far, he couldn't complain. But he had also stated that at the first sign of pilfering or wasting time, the culprit would be out on his ear. 'It's all in the genes, Randolph,' Jacob would say complacently. 'Just mark my words, because I know I'm right. In the end, none of them can possibly amount to much, not with their background.'

But it was always one special letter in the bundle which Randolph would keep to read last. Not that he needed to read it because he knew it off by heart. The writing was childish but perfectly formed and confident. It read:

Dear Mr Garfield,

   I am seven years old and I have been a Garfield orphan all my life. I have not had any other home, and I do not want one because I am very happy here even though the nuns get cross in the schoolroom sometimes and give us the cane.

   The only thing I want when I grow up is to get married and have my own house to keep clean, and my own children to look after. I have already met my husband, he is Mr Alexander, and I love him and I know he loves me because when he visits he always says he likes my dress and one day he said he thought my hair was a very pretty colour. He is a kind person so I know he would treat me well and not beat me like Ruby was beaten. Ruby is my best friend, and she is going to be my bridesmaid at the wedding.

   Thank you very much for all you give us at the Garfield Home. You are a kind person.

   I hope you are well. I am very well.

   Yours sincerely,

   Angelina Green

August 1914

Emma Kingston glanced at the calendar on her desk. The war, the much dreaded war, was now a month old, and so far all seemed to be quiet. Thoughtfully, she went across to the window and stared out, a shiver of dread running through her. Because surely this was just the calm before the storm. She knew it, felt it in her bones – after all, she studied the papers, listened to the wireless, heard the ranting of their politicians, the determination and intransigence of the unstoppable German invaders. The country, perhaps the whole world, was about to embark on a nightmare of indescribable horror.

And how many of the little orphans who had passed through her hands might be caught up in it, maimed, killed…

Presently, the superintendent popped her head around the school room door.

'Angelina, would you go to the sick room, please? The nurse could do with another pair of hands this morning. Oh, and after dinner, I would like to see you in my office for a few minutes.'

Angelina, who had been helping the younger children recite their times tables, turned at once to do as she'd been asked. If there was one place she loved best in the world to be, it was in the medical room at the far end of the corridor. For the last couple of days there had been a sickness bug going about and the current young nurse, Greta, always asked for Angelina, who, Greta had said more than once, had a natural understanding of what needed to be done and a gift for reassuring the little patients and making them feel safe. But Emma Kingston had realised this talent for a long time, and it had clearly been proved when a little waif – later known as Ruby – had been brought in from the streets, half-naked and badly bruised. For many weeks the poor child had not uttered a single word, keeping her eyes and mouth tightly shut, and even now, after so many years had passed, the superintendent's anger rose in her throat at the memory of that little one's distress. Not even her own kindly experience had been able to make the child talk. But Angelina had taken the little girl under her wing, reading Peter Pan and Wendy to her, over and over again, and letting her share and cuddle Angelina's precious pink teddy as they were in bed together. So when one day the little voice had finally whispered 'My name is Ruby', it had seemed as if Angelina had performed a small miracle.

Now, Angelina tapped on the superintendent's door and went in. Emma Kingston looked up. This child – no longer a child – had developed into a beautiful young woman. She had grown quite tall, with a willowy figure that seemed full of grace and energy, and her long, golden brown hair falling in soft waves around her face, always shone with health,

'Ah, there you are, dear. Come and sit down for a few minutes because we've one or two things to discuss.'

Angelina sat at the other side of the desk and looked across. 'Is there something you need me to do, Miss Kingston?'

'No, it's more about you, dear, and what's ahead.' She cleared her throat. This was one of the duties she never enjoyed. 'I don't need to remind you that in a few months you will be 14 years old,' she went on, 'and that in January you will be leaving us and moving on to pastures new.'

Angelina sat forward and smiled. 'You mean that I must make space for another child to come and live at The Garfield?'

'Yes, I am afraid so, and if I had my way you would all stay on here for ever!' the superintendent said. 'But as you know 14 has always been the leaving age, and Mr Garfield, too, is of the opinion that all children should be encouraged to make their own way in the world and accept responsibility for themselves. But he also insists that the door is never closed to any of you and that you are welcome to come and visit as often as you like.'

She looked away for a moment, not wanting to admit that parting with Angelina was going to be hard. She had always been a special child, a favourite child. And why should she not be, because it was thanks to her arrival fourteen years ago that the orphanage had been transformed, or that it even existed in this place. The day that Randolph Garfield had turned up, holding that little shoe box, had been a red-letter day for all of them, and if someone else had found the baby this orphanage would now be an empty shell. Instead, under his ownership, new lighting and heating had been installed straightaway, there were now two bathrooms upstairs, the kitchen had been refitted with new equipment and every room was regularly redecorated in bright colours. Not only those practical considerations had been attended to, but there was always a continuous supply of new books and toys and games – the Meccano sets brought in a few years ago proving an endless fascination for both girls and boys.

It seemed that Mr Garfield was determined to leave no stone unturned for his orphans, often employing extra tutors to help any child with difficulties, or who showed a talent or willingness to learn. Mr Garfield regularly came in to visit, often bringing his young son with him, and it always surprised Emma Kingston that their benefactor was very good at remembering most of the children's names. But he never again referred to Angelina's sad beginning, nor treated her differently from the others. In fact, discussion about any of the orphans was discouraged at the Home. The totally unknown were baptised and given simple Christian names, and told that their parents had died, that they were all in the same boat and the past was the past. The future, their future, was what mattered. The superintendent sighed happily at her own thoughts. Ten years ago she should have retired, but she was still here at the Garfield, and had never been more content with her lot.

'I shall be very sorry to leave,' Angelina said, 'because I have always been so happy here.' She smiled. 'Though I am sure the nuns will be glad to see the back of me, especially Sister Bernadette because she's never forgiven me for calling out that she'd given us the wrong answer to one of the sums in a test. I got caned

23

for that because she said I was being very rude in challenging her authority.'

Emma Kingston smiled briefly. She knew the nuns often used the cane on the children's outstretched hands, and although she did not approve of physical punishment there was little she could say. The orphanage was fortunate to have the support of the priory, and of the nuns, who came over each day. This was an arrangement which had always gone on, and it was part of the agreement with Father Laurence who still remained a nominal trustee. But the superintendent didn't care much for the priest who came in far too often for her liking. After all, once prayers and the reading of the day and perhaps a hymn had taken place, there wasn't that much for the man to do, but he usually made sure he was around to join them at mealtimes. He was very tall and gaunt, always dressed in his long black garb, and he rarely smiled.

'And I know someone else who won't be sorry that I'm going,' Angelina went on. 'Mrs Marshall! She will be very glad to see the back of me! For as long as I can remember she's told me to shut up and make myself scarce!'

Angelina looked away for a moment, not wanting to remember that one horrible event between her and Mrs Marshall that had given her nightmares for weeks afterwards.

It had been a day not long after Angelina's tenth birthday, when both the ovens in the kitchen had stopped working. Such a thing had never happened before, and for two days the orphanage had had to buy in their dinner from outside caterers. At midday, a white delivery van had arrived at the entrance, and Mrs Marshall had been there to receive the food and carry it inside, helped by one of the children. It had been on the second day that Mrs Marshall had called Angelina out from the school room to assist her.

'Hurry up,' the woman had said crossly, as the two had made their way down the long passageway. 'That van won't wait there for ever!'

'I am hurrying up,' Angelina had replied, annoyed that she'd had to leave the arithmetic lesson, her favourite. She'd trotted after Mrs Marshall. 'I can't walk any faster! Your legs are longer than mine, remember!'

'Always ready with a reply, aren't you, Miss!' Mrs Marshall had said. 'I wish I'd been born with even half of *your* cheek!'

At the entrance, the van had been there, ready and waiting. The driver entered and, one, by one, had placed three large, rectangular, shiny steel pans of hot food on the table in the hall. Then he'd touched his cap and was gone.

Mrs Marshall had gingerly lifted the lid from each pan, and she and Angelina had gazed at the contents. The first had held slice after slice of beef, accompanied by rows and rows of crisp, roast potatoes, all lying in a generous amount of rich brown gravy. The smell had made Angelina's mouth water.

'Can we pinch a spud?' she'd whispered, only to be rewarded with a clip over the ear.

The next pan had held cabbage and diced carrots, and in the third were the puddings, tiny jam roly polys, with a deep space at the end of the pan to hold the hot custard.

'Come on, let's get this lot into the kitchen before it all goes cold!' Mrs Marshall had said tersely, picking up the heaviest pan with the meat and potatoes inside. 'You bring the vegetables, Angelina. And don't dawdle!'

The next few moments were to be the ones imprinted on Angelina's memory for the rest of her life.

With Mrs Marshall going ahead, they'd been making their way along the corridor towards the kitchen, when suddenly the older woman had lost her grip on her hot pan and it fell to the floor with an ear-deafening crash, spilling the contents all over the place. And lying there in front of their horrified eyes, were the precious meat and potatoes, all floating in the gravy – which had begun swirling around and creeping into the cracks and corners of the stone floor.

25

For a few seconds neither of them spoke, then Angelina had put her own pan down on the floor and began trying to salvage some of the wasted food, just as Mrs Haines, hearing the commotion, had begun hurrying from the kitchen.

'What on earth is going on!' the cook had demanded. 'Oh my Good Lord…' she'd said on seeing the mess. 'Whatever are we going to do now!'

'That was all Angelina's fault!' Mrs Marshall had declared shrilly, her voice ringing through the corridor, 'She is such a *stupid* child! I told her to be careful, but she would insist on carrying the heaviest pan! She thinks she knows everything, can do everything better than anyone else and it's time someone taught her a lesson!'

For once, Angelina had been speechless. How *could* she be accused of something that was not her fault? How *could* Mrs Marshall be so horrible?

Trying to stem her tears, Angelina had just stared unbelievingly at Mrs Marshall. 'But I wasn't holding that pan! You know I wasn't!' Angelina had spluttered. 'You dropped it, not me! It's not fair to say it was me!'

But she was to get no further because just then Emma Kingston had appeared.

'Oh dear,' the superintendent had said as she'd surveyed the scene. 'Never mind, we must make do as best we can – it's too late to order a replacement, but I'm sure we can deal with this.' She had lifted the lid from the other pan. 'Look, we still have the vegetables and the puddings must be in that other one back there on the table, so all is not lost and perhaps marmite sandwiches will fill the gap, just for once.'

'I *told* Angelina to be careful!' Mrs Marshall had declared, determined to maintain the fallacy, 'but you can't tell her! Oh no. This one always knows best!'

'Never mind,' Emma Kingston had said. 'Accidents do happen now and again.' She'd glanced briefly at Angelina. 'Perhaps you

26

will help Mrs Marshall clean this up, Angelina, and then come and have your own dinner. Mrs Haines and I will take the other pans to the kitchen and prepare the tables. Everyone will soon be getting hungry!'

Then, Mrs Marshall had gone to the kitchen to fetch a large bowl, and soap and water and cloths, and between them, she and Angelina had picked up all the beautiful potatoes, one after another, and the slices of meat, and had washed the floor until all that remained of the event was a large, black stain which would soon dry up and disappear, leaving no trace that anything had happened.

But what would not disappear, ever, was Angelina's memory of the occasion. As she and Mrs Marshall had knelt there together on the floor, not another word had passed between them. Because what would have been the point? The older woman had told a direct lie to save her face, and as an adult, her version of the accident would be the one believed if Angelina had decided to say anything to the superintendent or Mrs Haines. But it had taught Angelina one of the hardest lessons in life – that adults are quite capable of telling downright lies, and justice does not always prevail.

At the end of the evening, with everything completed, she'd stood up and gazed into Mrs Marshall's unflinching eyes – only to see a look of triumph. The woman had got herself off the hook.

Mrs Marshall, while carrying all the cleaning materials back into the kitchen, had breathed a sigh of relief. Mrs Haines, the matriarch of the domestic staff, would have had a few choice words to say to her if she had known the truth. The cook had a quick tongue and was ready to criticise the others in her domain when things went a bit wrong, and there had been one or two small incidents recently that had put Mrs Marshall on the wrong foot.

Mrs Marshall had shrugged to herself. Anyway, Miss Angelina Green, the Miss Who Can Do No Wrong, would come to no harm over being accused. Oh no, *she* wouldn't get told off. Besides, Mrs

Marshall loved it here at the Garfield and couldn't afford to lose this job. The money was good, and she had a sick husband to feed and take care of.

Besides, who cared about a child's sensitivities? Children got over things pretty quickly.

Later that night, lying next to Ruby who was sleeping soundly, Angelina had wished with all her heart that she could tell Mr Alexander about what had happened. He would understand and sympathise with her, she knew he would, because each time he visited he always made a point of seeking her out so that they could have their lovely chats together. Mr Alexander was the sort of person you could say anything to, and Angelina had known that he would be as cross with Mrs Marshall as she was.

Now, almost four years later, the superintendent nodded at Angelina's remark that the girl believed Mrs Marshall had never liked her. Emma Kingston had always been aware of the woman's short temper – especially, it seemed, with Angelina who, from such an early age had been so bright, so clever, so quick to catch on. Perhaps Mrs Marshall was actually jealous of the child's ability in the schoolroom, because she herself was not well educated. In fact, little was known about the woman because she never discussed her personal life other than to say that she lived near the docks with her ailing husband. But she was a good worker and always came in on time, and over the years had introduced one or two other women, neighbours of hers, who needed casual employment, and so far all had proved more than satisfactory. Emma Kingston had found this useful, because she preferred to engage recommended staff.

'Well, we can't be liked by everyone in this world, can we, Angelina?' the superintendent said cheerfully. 'And make no mistake, you are dearly loved by all the rest of us.' Now then—' she looked down at the folder on her desk '—we shall naturally find you suitable accommodation after you leave here, and I am sure that it will not be difficult to find you work so this is what I want us to talk about. Do you have any particular wishes? You are a very competent girl in so many ways, dear – so, for example, I am certain you would be welcome to learn a trade in one of the hotels or guest houses. You might even like to learn more about cookery because you seem very happy in the kitchen helping Mrs Haines. Apart from washing up and keeping the place clean, she's told me that you are quick at peeling vegetables and very good at rubbing up short crust pastry!'

'Yes, I do like being in the kitchen,' Angelina said. 'Mrs Haines has taught me a lot.'

'Or maybe you would like to think about office work,' the superintendent went on. 'Perhaps Mr Garfield knows of someone who could do with a young clerk.' She glanced at Angelina quickly. 'Of course, everyone has to start at the bottom and you will not earn very much at the beginning.'

'I wouldn't mind that, Miss Kingston,' Angelina said.

'Of course, there are still a few months to go yet, before we need take any action, but do any of my suggestions appeal to you, Angelina? Or do you have thoughts of your own?'

Angelina took a deep breath. 'Miss Kingston, I know exactly what I am going to do with my life.'

The superintendent looked up, unsurprised at this. Angelina had had her feet very firmly on the ground from the moment she had taken her first steps.

'Go on.'

'I am going to train to be a nurse,' Angelina said emphatically, and without stopping for breath she went on. 'I have been thinking so much about it, and talking to Greta, and she's told me that St Thomas's have a nurses' training school and that anyone can apply and I know I'm a bit young but next year I shall be going on fifteen and that's how old they'll take you and I know I can be a good nurse because I've helped in the medical room for a long time now, haven't I? Nancy is a ward sister at the hospital now, and she could tell them about me and explain that I work hard and that the sight of blood doesn't upset me – I know what to do with damaged knees and bumped heads – and I don't mind cleaning up sick—'

Emma Kingston raised her hand and smiled. 'Well then, I think we shall have to make some enquiries about this Angelina, and if you think it is really what you want.'

'I *know* it's what I want, Miss Kingston!' Angelina said. 'I've read all about Miss Florence Nightingale and what a wonderful woman she was and I can't wait to learn everything and wear a nurse's uniform and—'

'You may have to wait a while, my dear,' the superintendent said, 'because you are still very young. But this is certainly something to be thinking about, isn't it?'

Angelina looked away for a moment. 'There is something that is worrying me, Miss Kingston,' she said, 'and it's about Ruby. You see, she has no idea that I've got to leave next year and she's going to be upset. Do you think she could leave at the same time and then we could go and live together? And I could go on looking after her, couldn't I?'

The superintendent glanced at her folder again. 'Well, we don't know how old Ruby actually is,' she said, 'but we are fairly certain that you and she are about the same age. So I think that what you suggest could be possible, and I, personally, would be happy that you would be around to keep an eye on her. But of course, she would have to be prepared to support herself, and it may be difficult to find work for her. She is a very sensitive young girl.'

Angelina was overjoyed. She couldn't bear to think of Ruby crying herself to sleep without their teddy bear to cuddle.

Emma Kingston stood up. 'Well, you've certainly given me something to think about, Angelina, so we will leave this for the moment'

Angelina stood as well. 'I feel really excited that you agree with my plan,' she said. 'Even though I am going to miss you all, miss everything when I go. Everyone has taught me things. I mean,

30

people like Mrs Haines, and Nancy when she was here and now Greta – and Miss Jones who is so sweet and kind to all of us and very patient. She was the one who taught us cross stitch and do those patterned squares that we sewed up to make a blanket for the doll's cot, and she helped Ruby to draw all the flowers that are in the nature books. Ruby loves flowers, knows the names of every one of them.'

'Ah yes,' Emma Kingston said. Maria Jones, one of Mrs Marshall's 'finds', had been here for many years on and off, and was always ready to step in when needed.

Before they left the room, Angelina said sadly, 'Once I do leave, I don't suppose I shall ever see much of Mr Garfield again or Mr Alexander, either. He's usually at college now, of course, but he's always made me feel I was someone special. When I was small I was in love with him and used to pretend that I was Cinderella and he was my Prince Charming.'

The superintendent's eyes softened. From the moment that Angelina had seen Randolph Garfield's son it had been obvious that she was enchanted. Each time he'd come to the orphanage, the handsome young lad treated her with the sort of attentive and gallant behaviour typical of a well-bred male of the upper crust – even when he'd brought his pretty and vivacious girlfriend Honora Mason with him. It was enough to turn any girl's head.

Emma Kingston pressed her lips together. She herself knew what it was to care deeply for someone who would never be within her reach.

As Angelina opened the door for Miss Kingston to go in front of her, she said, 'Do you know, of all the orphans, it's going to be the tiny ones I shall really miss – the 4- and 5-year-olds. I would like them all to come and live with me!'

'Well, you may have tiny ones of your own one day, my dear,' the superintendent said, 'and I am sure you will be a wonderful mother.'

'Oh, I am never going to get married,' Angelina said firmly. 'Not now. Not since I've decided to become a nurse.'

'Well, try and be patient about that, my dear,' Miss Kingston said. 'You are still very young, and you might have to wait a while for your dream to come true. But whatever you do, Angelina, I have no doubt about one thing – you will always be the one right there in the front line.'

Chapter 4

March 1915

In his bedroom at the priory, Laurence Dunn rose slowly from his knees, crossed himself, murmured a silent prayer and yawned. It was barely daylight, and looked to be another cold, grey morning. Another day like yesterday, and the day before, and the day before that.

Sighing, he washed and shaved – taking great care not to nick his skin – then brushed his teeth, and got dressed, the ritual performed in exactly the same order every day. Because routine was the best thing. There was comfort in routine – as there was in doing one's duty. And he was satisfied that he had certainly done his – no, was still doing his. He celebrated Mass twice every day at the priory, heard regular confessions, led the nuns in prayer, visited the sick and dying in the parish and had been a trustee at the orphanage for many years. It was he who made sure that every child who passed through the place during his time knew the Ten Commandments by heart, all the thou shall not do this or that, and those other things. Thanks to him, every orphan knew how to behave in life. That was something to take

33

away with them, surely? And Laurence Dunn admitted that he thoroughly enjoyed being part of the orphanage, especially since it had become the Garfield.

His accommodation, though sparse, was comfortable enough, and, recently, he had purchased a new mirror to go above the sink – well, the one that had been there for ages had yellowed so that he could barely see himself. But this replacement was bigger and longer, so that when he took a few steps back he could see much more of his appearance.

The priest was tall and spare-framed, his dark hair brushed away from a prominent forehead. But it was his black, glittering eyes and well-defined eyebrows that immediately caught the attention. He gazed back at himself with a certain amount of pride – one of the seven deadly sins, true, but it wasn't his fault that he was good-looking. If only fate – or rather his father – had allowed him to pursue another career, Laurence Dunn was certain that his name would be known to thousands, thousands. He would be famous, adored, respected.

He stood back, struck a pose, and raised his arm in a sweeping gesture.

'Friends, Romans, countrymen, lend me your ears! I come to bury Caesar, not to praise him!' he announced to the stone walls of his room. This was one of the speeches in a Shakespeare play that he never tired of, and he could complete it right to the end. And sometimes, if feeling melancholy, he enjoyed curling his tongue around other of the Bard's immortal words. 'No matter where, of comfort no man speak, let's talk of graves, of worms, of *epitaphs.*' The final word was pronounced with a menacing growl.

Laurence Dunn was entranced with the theatre and went to as many performances as time and money allowed. The stage, the smell, the atmosphere – the escape! *He* could have been one of those extraordinary players, those masters of the art! He could, he knew he could!

He completed the speech – which took quite a long time – and

34

bowed to the silent applause, taking several curtain calls. Then he felt cross with himself for indulging in this regular exercise because it didn't help. He had been planted in the priesthood and that would be that until he died. He was 45 years old and surely mature enough to accept what could not be changed, but he just wished he could rid himself of the cancerous envy he felt about his brother. Envy, another of those seven deadly sins...

Ernest was the younger by three years and had been allowed to do what he liked with his life. Their father, also a priest and of very high esteem, had been a domineering man and had commanded Laurence to follow him in Holy Orders, while Ernest had been allowed to look around and try one thing after another. For a very short time he had dabbled in the law, and even tried his hand at military service – though that didn't last, much too uncomfortable – and in the end Reverend Dunn senior gave up on his younger son and retired to his study to dwell on higher things. Which was all very well, but how had Ernest managed to survive all these years without a proper job? He lived in the West End in a rather nice house by all accounts, though Laurence had never been there, and on the odd occasion that the two brothers met up, Ernest seemed quite well-to-do. Smartly dressed, he always insisted on paying for their meal or their drinks, which was something. Laurence didn't like to ask where Ernest got his money from, but he had a good idea. Gambling. It was the only explanation, especially as once he'd said to Laurence, 'You backed the wrong horse, old boy.'

Now, Laurence checked once more on his appearance, and prepared to go over to the orphanage for breakfast. He enjoyed breakfast – well, he enjoyed everything which Mrs Haines produced – and after that he would be there to give God's blessing to two little girls who were leaving today.

*

Emma Kingston was not feeling at all well. She had slept badly and had woken with a headache. Why today, of all days – but perhaps it was the significance of the day which was causing her upset.

Angelina Green, their little throw-out orphan, was leaving the Garfield for the last time. Of all the children who had been part of her life, the superintendent was already feeling an acute sense of loss, because however much you spoke of coming back and of keeping in touch, she knew this was the parting of the ways, the end. It was the natural sequence of events, but each time it felt like a small bereavement.

She scolded herself at her thoughts. The young girl was more than ready to face the world and was longing to strike out on her own, taking Ruby with her. As it happened, their departure had been postponed by a few months because the room that had been found for them hadn't been ready. But now, after a few goodbyes to their friends, they would be making their way to their new home. When it was time for any of the orphans to leave, nothing special was made of the occasion except that Father Laurence always joined them for breakfast, and to give them a blessing to send them on their way. And on the final evening, Vera Haines always made cakes for tea, ensuring that there were enough left to make a small parcel for the departing children to take away with them.

Emma Kingston got dressed, took two more of her tablets, and sat down heavily on the bed. It was no good, this migraine was not going to leave her until much later – or even until tomorrow. For the first time in many years she would not be accompanying the children as they left. Someone else would have to do it – but not Mrs Marshall, the superintendent decided at once, even though the woman had done this twice before. No. The name that immediately sprang to mind was Maria Jones. She had a gentle way with the children and seemed especially fond of little Ruby.

*

In their warm coats and hats, and each carrying a suitcase containing their clothes and few belongings, Angelina and Ruby made their way along the street towards the bus stop, with Maria Jones walking alongside, also carrying a suitcase that held sheets and pillows and towels. She smiled down at them.

'What an exciting day this is for you!' she exclaimed. 'A new beginning!'

'I can't wait to see where we're going to be living!' Angelina exclaimed. 'Miss Kingston told me that it is very nice, and only a bus ride away from the orphanage, She said that she will be coming to see us as soon as she's better.'

'And you will be able to come and see us, won't you?' Maria Jones said. 'You must tell us what you're doing, and how you are getting on as working girls!'

Ruby, who'd been rather quiet, spoke up. 'I hope I shall know what to do at the salon,' she said, 'and that I don't knock things over and get in the way.'

'Ruby!' Angelina said firmly. 'Don't be a silly billy! Of course you won't! People will love you because you are careful and quiet and ready to do anything asked of you. It will be *interesting*, Ruby, and you will meet all sorts of different people.'

Ruby was going to be an assistant at a small, local hairdresser's salon, sweeping up and keeping things tidy for the manager and making tea for clients waiting under the huge machines for their hair to dry. Luckily, the place was quite near the small hotel where Angelina was to be employed as a general domestic help. Their combined wages would be just a few shillings, but enough to pay the rent for their room in the three-storey house, and for their food – if they were careful. Emma Kingston always took great trouble to see that her children would be as comfortable as possible in their new lives, and, fortunately, Garfield orphans were usually easy to place. People trusted the Garfield. This could be partly due, the superintendent sometimes thought, to Father Laurence's dramatic exhortations regarding bad behaviour and its consequences. She smiled inwardly. She knew that Mrs Marshall had no time for the man at all, and had several times intimated that she knew something suspicious about him. Oh yes, you wouldn't believe it, not from a man of the Cloth. But since Emma Kingston never indulged in any discussion or gossip about her staff or anyone connected with the orphanage, Mrs Marshall's secret remained just that. A secret.

Presently, arriving at the large Victorian building, Maria Jones ushered them inside the room on the ground floor which was to be the girls' new home.

'Now – what do you think of this!' she said cheerfully. 'Isn't it cosy and light?' She had already been to check out the place with Emma Kingston, who had come to value the younger woman's opinion.

Angelina was immediately enthusiastic. 'Look, Ruby, we've each got a bed now! And this little table by the window is where we shall have our meals, and these two soft chairs are where we can relax after our hard day at work. We are going to be very happy here, I know we are – especially as the landlord has lit our fire to welcome us! What more could we want?'

Maria Jones smiled. It was she who had been asked by Miss Kingston to come here earlier to make sure the room was warm when the two youngsters arrived. 'Look, the small sink here is for your immediate needs,' Maria Jones said, 'and outside in the yard is the coal house, and the lavatory and bath. You will be sharing with the people on the next floor – a young couple with a tiny baby.' She went on, 'Apart from your fireplace where you can boil a kettle, there's a stove on the first landing for you to do any cooking – also a communal one, but I'm sure you will manage.'

'Oh, of course we will manage!' Angelina exclaimed. 'We've been sharing with others all our lives – haven't we, Ruby? We're orphans, we're used to sharing.'

Ruby, who had said very little, looked pensive. 'I've never had a bed to myself,' she said slowly. 'I hope I shall be able to get to sleep on my own.'

'Don't worry about that,' Angelina said at once. 'You can always get in beside me until you drift off, and then I'll transfer you!' She squeezed Ruby's arm. 'It's all right, Ruby, there'll still always be the three of us – you, me and teddy.'

After they had made up the beds, and found out where the kettle and the cups and plates and cutlery were stored, Maria Jones went to the door.

'I had better go,' she said, 'because I must report back to Miss Kingston.' She smiled. ''And I shall tell her that I think you are going to be very happy here.'

Much, much later, with Ruby snuggled in beside her and fast asleep, Angelina's mind was churning with all the hopes and thoughts and ambitions that wouldn't leave her alone. She knew that, for the moment, her life had been set out for her and that she must accept it. She was lucky to have been found a job, and the owner of the hotel had treated her very kindly at the interview, though the woman in charge of the kitchen where Angelina would be working hadn't seemed so keen. She'd stared at Angelina suspiciously and had refused Angelina's offer to shake her hand, turning away curtly. But that didn't bother Angelina, who had no intention of being there very long in any case. She had already made up her mind about her next step. In August she would be applying to St Thomas's to join their nursing school. She was already sorting out the details. She didn't think that she would be a live-in candidate at first, so she and Ruby would still be here together for a while, and after that, well… it was no good looking too far ahead. Things would work out. Angelina would make sure they did.

She turned over to face Ruby who was deeply asleep, and very carefully lifted the smaller child into her arms and moved the few steps to the other bed, and tucked her in. Ruby was still clutching the little pink teddy bear, and Angelina didn't have the heart to take it from her. It was their first night away, after all.

After the excitement of the day, even Angelina was beginning to feel tired, which was unusual. She seldom felt tired because there was always so much to do. So much to think about.

In the quiet of that modest room, she let her imagination take her to that honeyed, secret place in her heart. A place she was visiting more and more.

She was here in bed with Alexander beside her. Her Prince Charming had claimed her as his own and she could feel his gentle, kind hands, could hear his deep voice murmuring sweet words.

'I love you, darling Angelina, with all my heart,' he murmured. 'You know I always have, and I always will.'

'I know that, Alexander, and I will always love you, too,' Angelina softly whispered the familiar words which she had said over and over to herself for so long, felt his caress, the beat of his heart against her own, his requesting lips on hers. And she murmured again, 'I know I can never be yours, Alexander, but I will love you until the end of my days.'

Chapter 5

For the first few weeks, life did seem strange to both the girls, because for the first time in their young lives they had to work out their own routines. To get up in time without being told – and go to bed when they felt like it – to sort out their clothes, and their mealtimes, and keep their room clean without it being checked up on by Mrs Marshall or Miss Jones.

Before they were to start work, Angelina and Ruby had been given three days to get used to everything, and to find their way around their new neighbourhood. On the first morning, straight after breakfast, they went out to do a little shopping.

Dressed in their warm hats and coats, because it was still very cold, they left the house and started walking towards a small row of shops at the far end of the long street.

The first one they came to was the greengrocer's, which had the name 'Foster's' in big letters above the door. Already displayed outside were ranks of vegetables, all neatly set out. Potatoes and carrots and parsnips and onions, and opposite, at the other side of the entrance, were baskets of tomatoes and apples, pomegranates and oranges. Ruby looked up at Angelina.

'Anybody could steal all this,' she whispered, 'because no one is looking after it, are they?'

Just then, the owner appeared at the door. He was a middle-aged man, dressed in a long white apron down to his knees, and with a jaunty white hat on his head. He smiled at the girls.

'Good morning, young ladies! Is there anything I can get you today?'

Both girls returned his smile. 'Oh, no thank you,' Angelina said, 'but I am sure we will be buying our vegetables from you very soon.' She hesitated, then said, 'You see, we have only just moved in – down the road in the big house at the end – and we have enough of everything for now. But thank you very much.'

The man grinned down at them. 'Well, welcome to the area, and I am sure you are going to be two of my best customers.' Then he picked out two rosy apples and two oranges and put them into a brown paper bag. 'Have these with my compliments,' he said as he turned to go back inside. 'I hope to see you again very soon.'

'Oh, *thank* you, Mr Foster,' Angelina said, 'that is so kind of you!'

Ruby, clutching the bag of fruit, looked at Angelina as the two walked towards the next shop. 'I thought we had to pay for everything,' she said.

'Of course we do, Ruby – usually – but not if it's a present.'

The next shop was the butcher's, outside of which were carcasses of lambs and pigs hanging on huge hooks. Ruby shuddered. 'I don't like the look of this,' she said. 'Those poor animals, Angelina.'

Angelina shoved Ruby ahead of her. 'Well, don't look, Ruby. Now here's the newsagent's – and there are sure to be sweets! Come on, we haven't spent anything yet, so we can afford to buy some toffees. We both like those, don't we?'

Walking on slowly, they passed the hardware shop and the grocer's, and finally they came to the baker's. The smell of freshly cooked bread was enough to make them stop and enter. Even though they had enough food in their cupboard to be going on with, they both decided they could afford to buy a currant bun each, to eat *now*. At last they retraced their steps and began making their way back home.

'I think I am going to really like living here, don't you, Ruby?' Angelina said, licking sugar from her fingers. 'Everyone is so kind and seems to like talking to us.'

Ruby nodded as she finished the last of her bun. 'And look over there, Angelina – I can see swings and see-saws. That must be a park over there, like the one we used to go to when we were at the Garfield.'

Angelina stared across. 'Yes, of course it's a park – and there are sure to be seats where we can sit when the weather gets warmer.'

There was silence for a few moments after that, with Angelina being acutely aware that, suddenly, her recent high spirits had dropped like a stone. And she knew it was because of that certain memory, two years earlier, which had refused to leave her, even though it was childish and silly.

It had been a lovely Saturday afternoon over Easter, and they had all gone to the park in the care of Miss Jones. Unusually, Miss Kingston had accompanied them as well. Everyone was especially happy because, after all, they had a week's holiday from school, and each child had received a big Easter egg, with smaller ones inside, some of which they'd taken with them to eat in the park.

Angelina and Ruby had been swinging contentedly together, side by side, to and fro, when in the near distance but away from the play area, Angelina had suddenly spotted two figures she'd recognised only too well. On one of the long benches beneath a huge sycamore tree, Alexander had been sitting there with Honora Mason. Beautiful Honora, his girlfriend. He'd had his arm around her shoulders and was looking down at her, and she was gazing up at him and smiling. Every now and then she would laugh her tinkling little laugh and she'd seemed so happy, so sure of herself and of what her future held.

Angelina's mouth had suddenly gone completely dry as she'd witnessed the scene. For her, the afternoon had been completely

43

ruined. She'd known she was being silly, because everyone knew that those two had always been meant for each other, and that one day they were sure to get married. But as long as Angelina didn't actually see them together, she could put that thought from her mind, could pretend that it wasn't true, after all. But that day, she couldn't deny the sight of her own eyes, and it was no good. She had never had any real chance of being anything more to the man of her dreams than one of his father's orphans whom he'd taken it into his head to be especially kind to. And had she been making *that* up, all this time, thinking she was someone special? Because he'd talked to other children as well, had seemed to take a real interest in what they were doing. Why had she allowed herself to fantasise that one day he would put that silver slipper on her foot and take her away to his palace and that they would live happily ever after?

She'd stopped swinging and Ruby had stopped too. 'Are you going to eat one of your chocolates now, Angelina?' Ruby had said.

'No,' Angelina had replied. 'I just don't feel like one, Ruby.'

'Have you got a tummy ache?' Ruby had asked as she'd started carefully removing the silver paper from one of the little eggs in her pocket.

'Not a tummy ache,' Angelina had replied, 'but I want to go home, now. I hope it's nearly time.'

As they'd all trooped back, Angelina had heard Miss Kingston talking to Miss Jones about Honora Mason and about what a lovely girl she was. And wasn't it charming to see two young people so much in love?

Now, as they were strolling back home, Angelina tried to shake off her pointless memories. She glanced down at Ruby. 'Isn't Miss Kingston clever to have found us somewhere like this to live, Ruby? I know it's a very long street and the grey houses look exactly the same – all those windows like beady eyes staring down at us are a little bit threatening! But it already begins to feel like home. It really does. Do you feel like that, too, Ruby?'

''Course I do,' Ruby said, tucking her hand into Angelina's arm. 'As long as we're both here together, anywhere will always feel like home.'

Angelina didn't say any more, thinking that one day soon, Ruby would have to get used to being a bit more by herself. Because a day didn't pass without Angelina envisaging herself dressed in a nurse's uniform...

But before that, next week, she must start working at the hotel, and the idea didn't appeal. It seemed such a waste of time when she could be starting on her proper career. But as Miss Kingston had advised, Angelina must be patient. She was still very young – perhaps too young – for St Thomas's to take her.

Angelina narrowed her eyes at her own thoughts. Just you wait, St Thomas's. However hard you try, you won't keep Angelina Green away. Not for long.

Chapter 6

It was Friday a few weeks later, and at six o'clock the salon was about to close for the day. Angelina was waiting outside to walk back home with Ruby. Angelina's hours at the hotel varied, and this week, she had finished early each day.

Presently, Ruby emerged. She ran over to Angelina, and they started walking back home.

'I was given three tips today, Angelina' Ruby exclaimed. 'Three! At this rate we are going to be rich!'

'Well, people don't give tips unless they are pleased with you,' Angelina said, 'so you must be doing everything right – as I always knew you would.'

'But I don't think I'll be allowed to do any shampooing and setting,' Ruby said. 'I mean, I knew I would be expected to sweep up and do chores, but now I speak to clients all the time – and they seem to like talking to me. Often, when I take them their tea, it's hard to get away! I don't want Mrs Walker to think I'm wasting time because she is so kind to me. She's even said she would teach me to do perms if I liked, but I don't think I will ever be as clever as she is. Imagine cutting hair with those sharp scissors! Whatever would I do if I took too much off! I couldn't put it back on again, could I!'

Angelina laughed. 'That could certainly be difficult,' she said, 'but you are doing brilliantly, Ruby, you really are. The best thing is, you are happy there, aren't you? You do look forward to going to work every day, don't you?'

Ruby didn't hesitate. 'I never thought I could be as happy as this – being away from the Garfield, I mean. Especially when Mrs Walker's husband sometimes pops in to bring fresh doughnuts for us to have in our tea break!'

Angelina looked at Ruby fondly, thinking how different it could have been if things had gone badly at the salon. Ruby's early life had left her with so many physical and emotional bruises she couldn't have taken much more.

'And have you had a good day too?' Ruby enquired.

Angelina made a face. 'As good as it will ever get, I think,' she said. 'It's not difficult work, of course, it's just *boring!* I'm not learning anything I didn't know before, and the woman in charge downstairs doesn't seem to like me one bit. She follows me around, checking up on whatever I'm doing, and it puts me on edge.' Angelina sighed. 'It's a good job that hotel work was only ever going to be a stop-gap until I become a nurse – unless the hospital doesn't think I'm good enough after all,' she added.

It was Ruby's turn to do the encouraging. 'Of course they won't think that, Angelina,' she said. 'They'll see straightaway that you are going to be a wonderful nurse! Look how you took care of me when I had all my funny attacks, and then when you were called to the sick room when some of us were all poorly at the same time! Everyone wanted you, Angelina, you know they did.'

As they arrived home, Angelina said, 'While I was waiting for you, I popped into the grocer's and bought some lovely ham – I watched while Miss Dawson sliced it off the bone, and even though I only asked for two slices she added an extra one because she said it had broken off and was too small and untidy to sell to another customer so we might just as well have it.'

Ruby smiled. 'Miss Dawson's ever so nice, isn't she Angelina?

When I pass the shops on my way to work she's often arranging things in the window and she always looks up and waves to me.'

Angelina nodded. 'Yes, she is very friendly – and so is Mr Foster. We knew that from our very first day, didn't we? I bought two tomatoes from him for us to have with our ham and he just wanted to chat and ask how we were getting on. Are you hungry, Ruby? We could have some mashed potatoes with our ham if you like.'

'I am not actually that hungry,' Ruby admitted, 'because Mr Walker turned up with doughnuts for us again. But I could manage just a few potatoes.'

'Okay, but don't forget we haven't got very long because we're looking after Nesta for Mr & Mrs Carter tonight.'

Alfred and Dora Carter were the young couple living on the first floor with their nine-month-old daughter, and as soon as Angelina and Ruby had met them they all knew they were going to get on. Which was just as well as they were sharing many of the amenities of the house. Mr Carter worked long hours at the docks and Mrs Carter took in ironing, but sometimes on a Friday evening the couple would go out for a drink together, leaving Nesta in the care of the girls. It was a happy arrangement and Angelina and Ruby loved having the baby to themselves, especially as Mrs Carter always left them to do the bath time ritual.

'I've been looking forward to it all day,' Ruby said, as they finished their tea. 'I was telling Mrs Walker about the lovely family that lives upstairs, and she said they'd always wished they'd had a daughter as well as a son.'

'Oh, I'd forgotten you'd said they had a son,' Angelina said. 'Does he ever come into the salon?'

'Well, I've never seen him,' Ruby replied. 'He's away at college apparently.'

With their meal finished and the dishes cleared away, the girls went up to the first floor and tapped on the Carters' door. Straightaway Mrs Carter appeared – looking really pretty, Angelina thought. She was wearing a blue cotton dress and had

48

done her long hair up on top and her lips were painted a bright pink. She looked like a young girl and was obviously excited to go out on the town with her husband. She opened the door wide for the girls to come in.

'Ah, there you are,' she said. 'Nesta has had her tea, and as usual she has her last bottle before you settle her down. But it's bath time first and everything's ready for you.'

Angelina and Ruby followed Mrs Carter into the small sitting room where the baby was sitting on the floor playing with her toys. Seeing the girls, she immediately crawled over, gurgling excitedly.

'See how she loves seeing you!' Dora Carter said.

'And we love Nesta!' Angelina exclaimed, scooping the baby into her arms and holding her high up in the air. 'We are going to get wet in a minute, Nesta, aren't we, and we are going to have fun!'

Just then, Mr Carter emerged from the bedroom. A spare man with thinning hair, he was tidily dressed in black trousers and grey open neck striped shirt. He grinned at the girls.

'Oh good,' he said jovially. 'Thank you for allowing us to escape for a couple of hours!'

'We love looking after Nesta!' the girls chorused as they followed the couple to the door, and Angelina said, 'Don't worry if you're back late. We don't mind, do we, Ruby?'

'Of course not!' Ruby said, and Mrs Carter turned to smile at them.

'It's so lovely that we can go out knowing that our baby is in such safe hands,' she said. 'We really don't know what we'd do without you.' She paused. 'I mean, we had no idea who'd be coming to live downstairs, and when you two turned up it was as if we'd handpicked you ourselves!'

*

It was three weeks later that Angelina finally plucked up the courage to put her plan into action. At four-thirty, after she'd

49

finished her shift for the day, she hurried back home to prepare herself for what lay ahead.

She washed, brushed out her hair – tying it firmly back from her face – then slipped into her straight black skirt, which she always wore with her cream, long-sleeved blouse. She didn't have many clothes to choose from and considered that this rather formal outfit might be suitable for coming face to face with the almoner at the hospital.

On arriving, she made her way to the entrance and was greeted straightaway by the uniformed commissionaire.

'What can I do for you, young lady?' he enquired, and Angelina smiled up at him, hoping he didn't notice her flushed cheeks. Her heart had been racing ever since she'd got off the bus.

'I would like to see the almoner, please sir,' she said, 'because I wish to become a nurse.' She swallowed nervously. 'I want to come here to the training school.'

The man stared down at her, not smiling.

'The almoner is a very busy lady, but I will see if she is available,' he said. 'What name shall I say?'

'Miss Angelina Green,' Angelina said, following him into his small office. As he picked up a telephone to make the call, she hugged herself with anticipation.

At least she had got this far! She was inside this amazing building, the very smell of which was already exciting her nostrils, the sounds and echoes and busy feet hurrying along corridors making her want to jump up and join in. This was where she wanted to be! She knew it was, and she knew she could be a good nurse if they would take her on.

But it was another half an hour before the telephone rang, after which the commissionaire rose from his desk and beckoned Angelina to follow him along an endless corridor to a room at the end.

'The almoner will see you now,' he said.

As Angelina entered the room, the almoner – a tall, middle-aged lady with short grey hair – stood up and greeted her kindly.

'Come in, Miss Green,' she said, 'and take a seat. My name is Miss Day, and I understand that you wish to enroll in our nurses' training school.'

'Oh, yes please,' Angelina said quickly. 'I have set my heart on it, because I know I could be a good nurse if I was properly trained.'

'Do you indeed?' the almoner said. 'Well then, let me have a few details. How old are you?'

This was the question Angelina had been dreading and she cleared her throat. 'I am fifteen… I think,' she said.

The almoner looked up, her eyebrows raised. 'You *think* you are fifteen? Don't you know? Do you have your birth certificate with you?'

Angelina paused, then said 'I don't have a birth certificate,' she said slowly. 'I have never had one because… because I am an orphan, you see, and no one is actually sure of my age, or anything about me, not really.' Angelina crossed her fingers against the little white lie; if they knew she was still only fourteen she'd have no chance.

The almoner's eyes softened. There were so many – too many – displaced children in this city, in the world. 'So where were you brought up, Miss Green?' she said.

'At the Garfield. I am a Garfield orphan,' Angelina said simply. 'I have lived there all my life, and Miss Kingston, the superintendent, will tell you how good and reliable I was in the medical room where I was often asked to help the nurse in charge.'

The almoner nodded slowly, thinking that yes, this girl could be about fifteen, and she appeared confident and certain about what she wanted to do. But as well as that there was an honesty, a simple earnestness, which appealed.

'Tell me, Miss Green,' the almoner said, 'if you were to witness someone taken ill in the street, and you were asked to help, what would be your first reaction?'

'I would reassure the patient and tell him to stay calm and still because help was at hand,' Angelina said at once. 'Then I would make sure his airways were not blocked, and that there was no significant blood loss.'

The almoner was impressed at this quick response. 'And where did you learn all that?'

I used to ask our nurse, Nancy, questions all the time in the medical room,' Angelina replied, 'and she would always tell me anything I wanted to know. And then, Greta, the nurse who came after Nancy, did exactly the same. They always seemed to like explaining things to me and I used to write it all down and learn it by heart afterwards.' Angelina smiled quickly. 'They never said they were fed up with all my questions, but I expect they probably were. I'm afraid I have a habit of keeping on and on when I'm curious,' she added.

The almoner looked across at Angelina. Of all the interviews she had conducted, this was one likely to remain in her memory. She handed a notebook across the desk.

'Write down your full name and address – and your age,' she added, smiling. 'Together with the names of any relatives or close friends you may have.' There was a long pause, then she said, 'And I will speak to the senior nurse, and give her all your details and tell her that, all being well, you will be joining the September intake,' Miss Day added.

Angelina nearly fell off her chair with amazement. Had the almoner actually said that she, Angelina Green, would be joining the training school in just a few months' time? Or was she dreaming?

She stood up. 'Thank you, Miss Day,' she said. 'Thank you for giving me this chance. I promise I will be worthy of it.'

The almoner stood as well. 'I am sure you will,. Miss Green,' she said. 'Now then, the session will begin on the first Monday in September and you will present yourself to me on that day at eight o'clock. You will not be living in at first, but you will be given over-alls to wear – and later, of course, you will be in uniform. But not before you have attended a number of lectures,' she added, smiling.

If it had been the right thing to do Angelina could have flung her arms around Miss Day's neck. She had done it! Angelina Green had done it! She was going to be a nurse at St Thomas'!

The almoner came over and shook Angelina's hand. 'I can see that you are very happy to be joining us, Miss Green,' she said, 'but I hope you will not be too disillusioned at first.' She sighed briefly. 'Because of the present ghastly situation across the channel, nurses are needed more than ever. But nursing is a very hard job, the hours are long and arduous and the pay is small. A mere pittance. Not everyone manages to stay the course.'

'Oh, I will, Miss Day,' Angelina said. 'I never give up on anything I start.'

'I believe you, Miss Green,' the almoner said, following Angelina to the door.

Chapter 7

August 1915

In his study, Randolph Garfield tried to look forward to his friend's usual visit with more anticipation but was finding it difficult. Tonight Randolph would have preferred to be by himself.

The war was exactly one year old and all indications were that it was not going well. And he knew that Jacob Mason would have all the facts, ready with his opinions about who, and what, was responsible and how to solve the mess. Perhaps selfishly, the one fact that was weighing heavily on Randolph's mind was that Alexander was more than likely to become involved.

Randolph moved over to pour himself a brandy. With college closed for the summer break, Alexander was staying with Honora and her mother at their holiday cottage in Devon for a couple of weeks, and Randolph had accepted the invitation to join Jacob and the family for the coming weekend. Randolph wished he'd made some excuse not to go. He just didn't feel like it, not while young men were dying in the trenches, many even younger than Alexander, by all accounts.

Jacob duly arrived, and took his usual chair opposite Randolph, his white napkin on his knee ready to enjoy his plate of cold meats.

'Don't look so worried, Randolph,' Jacob said heartily. 'Kitchener knows what he's doing and I've got great faith in young Churchill. They'll sort it out between them and before you know it, all those brave lads will be coming home again.'

'You really think so, Jacob?' Randolph said quietly, not bothering to point out that among 'those brave lads' were certain to be many hopeless, rootless youngsters – Jacob's so-called 'driftwood' – for whom volunteering to sacrifice their lives might have seemed an escape, or even an exciting interruption to their sad and mundane existence.

'Well, you will forgive me,' Randolph went on, when I say that I fear for my son, Jacob. I have one son, one precious son, and I believe that conscription is to come into force next year which will include Alexander straightaway. Even if he doesn't volunteer beforehand, which he may well decide to do.'

'Oh, we must scotch that idea at once!' Jacob declared. 'Alexander is much too important to you – to us – Honora would be devastated! And as far as conscription is concerned, there are ways around that, Randolph. After all, you can declare that Alexander is essential to the economy, being heavily involved with the family firm, with Garfield Tobacco...'

'But he is not involved,' Randolph said. 'He is studying at college, and likely to be doing so for at least three more years. There is no reason why he should not be called up.'

Jacob held out his glass for a refill. 'Oh, let's not worry about that tonight, Randolph,' he said. 'Let's look forward to the weekend ahead! I've heard from Elizabeth that the weather is lovely down there and that our youngsters are having a wonderful time together, in and out of the water all the time! Well, they deserve it, don't they – with Alexander away so much. I know Honora misses him terribly when he's not with her – well, we all miss him of course, but for Honora it's different. Those two are meant to be together. Always were,' Jacob added firmly.

The following day Maria Jones tapped on the superintendent's door, and went in. Emma Kingston looked up from her desk, smiling.

'Oh, thank you for staying on, Miss Jones,' she said, 'and thank you, once more, for checking up on our little ex-orphans for me as you do.' She paused. 'I feel I have come to rely on you rather too much in this particular matter.'

'I am not nearly as busy as you are, Miss Kingston,' Maria Jones said, 'and when I leave here each day my time is my own, while you are always on duty, always on call. I sometimes wonder how you keep so cheerful all the time. And anyway, I do love visiting the young people, and making sure they're all right so it's no hardship,' she added.

'That's so good to hear,' Emma Kingston said, 'and don't worry about me, my dear. This place is where I'm rooted, and where I'm at my happiest. Now then...' She glanced at papers on her desk. 'Of the four who left us this year let's start with Joshua and Thomas. As far as you can tell, do you think that everything is still all right with them?'

'I think they are perfectly happy, safe and settled,' Maria Jones said. 'Well, there's been no complaint from either of the landlords, which is a good sign! And they both seem to like their jobs – especially on pay day! No – I think they're fine.'

The superintendent nodded, pleased. Over the years there had been one or two difficult youngsters who'd found it difficult to adjust to life outside the orphanage, but they were few and far between. Miss Kingston liked to think that that was because the door was never shut to the leavers, many of whom visited now and then if they needed help or advice about something, or if they just wanted to come back for tea. Wherever they went, they would always be her children and they knew it.

'And what about Angelina and Ruby?' Emma Kingston said, though she didn't really need to ask. She had gone to the house just after they'd moved in, and once again since, and it had been obvious that it was just right for those two.

'They are both very happy,' Maria Jones said at once, 'especially Ruby, who loves her job at the hairdresser's. Though Angelina isn't quite so keen on hers because she finds it tedious. But they like their room and they've made friends with the little family upstairs and look after their baby now and again – which they seem to love.'

The superintendent nodded. 'Give Angelina someone to look after and take care of and she's happy.' Emma paused for a second, before adding, 'I can't help thinking that Angelina's natural good-will emanates from appreciating her great fortune at having been rescued by Mr Randolph.'

Maria nodded her agreement at this suggestion, then turned to go. 'So that's it, Miss Kingston. You can set your mind at rest about those four,' she said. 'As far as I can tell, there is absolutely nothing to worry about.'

Emma Kingston stood up. 'I repeat, I am very grateful to you, Miss Jones,' she said. 'You are a very hard-working and loyal member of the staff, and I feel I can trust you with anything at all.'

'Thank you, Miss Kingston,' Maria Jones said. 'It was Mrs Marshall who introduced me, if you remember, and I feel privileged to be working at the Garfield.'

Just then they heard the doorbell ring, and the sound of Mrs Marshall's feet hurrying to answer it. Emma Kingston raised her eyes.

'Oh – I hope this is not a newcomer,' she said, 'because we simply don't have any room at the moment.'

But it was not a newcomer, and after tapping on the door, Angelina and Ruby burst in, all smiles.

'To what do we owe the pleasure?' Emma Kingston said, coming over to give them a hug.

'It's because I have some *news*!' Angelina exclaimed, 'Guess what? I've been taken on, Miss Kingston! At St Thomas's nurses' training school! I start in three weeks' time and I still can't believe it!'

'Well, well, well' Emma Kingston said. 'Do come in, sit down, and tell us all about it.

Mrs Marshall, who'd been hovering in the doorway full of curiosity, broke in. 'Would you like me to fetch you a pot of tea, Miss Kingston?' The superintendent nodded.

'What a good idea, Mrs Marshall – and no, don't go, Miss Jones. You must stay and hear what this is all about! We like exciting news!'

And hardly pausing for breath, Angelina described every detail of her interview at the hospital.

'I still feel that I'm dreaming,' she said, dipping her biscuit into her tea when it had arrived. 'Because it's a dream come true, you know it is, Miss Kingston.'

'Yes, we did discuss it last year, didn't we – but do they know that you are not quite fifteen?'

Angelina didn't flinch. 'Oh well, I said I *thought* I was but that I didn't really know, and anyway the almoner asked me all sorts of other questions about nursing and my ambitions and things like that. She seemed quite happy about everything so I don't think my age matters at all.' Angelina took another biscuit. 'And I am going to be paid while I'm training – a very small wage, I believe, but I don't mind about that. It will probably be enough to still pay my share of our rent, because I shan't be living-in for a long time, I don't think.'

Maria Jones poured everyone a second cup of tea, and looked across at Ruby who'd hardly uttered a word. 'And what do *you* think of all this Ruby?' she asked.

'I just think that Angelina will make the best nurse in the whole world,' Ruby said, 'because whatever she does, she's always out there in front of everyone else. And anyway, it doesn't matter if her wage is small because I have been given a rise in pay! Mrs Walker told me yesterday that she is very pleased with the way I have gained in confidence.' Ruby smiled broadly. 'I am going to be allowed to do some sets soon. I've stayed behind a couple of evenings each week so she could show me exactly how to do it. She says it won't take me long to get the hang of it because she thinks I have a natural flair for hairdressing.'

Emma Kingston felt a small rush of pride as she looked at Ruby, remembering the pitiful state the child was in when she arrived at the orphanage all those years ago. Now her life seemed to have blossomed, and she was looking so pretty in her flowery, printed cotton dress, with her fair hair – which had always been a rather unruly mass of tight curls – having been styled to follow the shape of her face.

'I do like the way you've done your hair, Ruby,' Emma Kingston said.

'That's thanks to Mrs Walker,' Ruby said, 'because almost as soon as I started at the salon she suggested I might like to do it this way. And every morning, before we open, we both do our hair ready for the day. We sit side by side in front of the mirrors, because as she often says – if we don't look good ourselves, we're hardly likely to encourage clients to come in.'

Emma Kingston sipped at her tea thoughtfully. The moment she had approached the owner of the hairdressing salon about giving young Ruby Lane a chance of some work, she'd been optimistic. Mrs Walker was clearly a kind and considerate woman, and had agreed to take the girl on for a couple of months to see if her work and attitude proved satisfactory. Since Emma Kingston had not heard another word it was obvious that Ruby had found her niche. Many of the orphans who left to live and work further away were seldom heard from again, so it always delighted the superintendent when her children stayed close enough for her to chart their progress.

'So, then, Angelina,' the superintendent said, 'when does the

Garfield's Florence Nightingale actually take out her thermometer?'

'Monday the sixth of September,' Angelina said happily. 'I told the hotel this morning that I must leave them on the Friday before so I've got the weekend to prepare myself for the medical world, but I don't think I'll be given a thermometer straightaway, Miss Kingston! For one thing, there are lectures to attend, and there'll be notes to write up and remember. And tests and exams!'

'Well, you will certainly enjoy that side of things,' Emma Kingston said, 'because you always loved your schoolwork, didn't you? But I'm sure you will soon be given more practical things to do as well. Patients to take care of, and that sort of thing.'

'Can't wait!' Angelina said.

*

After the girls had left, Mrs Marshall gathered up the tea things and returned to the kitchen. Vera Haines was finishing for the day, and she turned to look at Mrs Marshall.

'He's been at it again... the priest,' the cook said, lowering her voice.

'Never! Are you sure?' Mrs Marshall looked aghast.

'Of course I'm sure, and I think it's absolutely disgusting. I mean, a man in his position.'

Mrs Marshall shook her head slowly. 'This has been going on for too long, Mrs Haines, and I think something should be done about it. I mean – we should do something about it.'

'But it would be so embarrassing,' Vera Haines said slowly. 'I really don't think I could find the words.'

Mrs Marshall pursed her lips. 'Well, at least Miss Kingston should be told. She will know how to deal with this.'

'Oh, you know Miss Kingston,' Vera Haines said emphatically. 'She will never hear a bad word said about anyone, anyone at all. So she's not likely to believe us.'

Mrs Marshall sighed deeply. 'It's awful to feel so helpless, isn't it? I mean, what chance do people like us ever have of challenging someone like the priest? We're not in the same class.'

Vera Haines folded her arms. 'Still, I think it's absolutely disgusting and he should be thoroughly ashamed of himself.'

'I totally agree,' Mrs Marshall said, turning away. 'It's *disgusting*!'

As she opened the front entrance door to leave for the day, Mrs Marshall heard scurrying feet coming up behind her. It was Miss Jones, and soon, the two began walking home together. This rarely happened, because although they lived fairly close, Mrs Marshall worked later hours.

'Well, Angelina is certainly thrilled to be taken on at St Thomas's,' Mrs Marshall said, 'I hope the life comes up to her expectations. Nursing is not for everyone.'

Maria Jones nodded. 'No, you are right, Mrs Marshall, but I really believe that it is perfect for Angelina, and I think she is going to do very well. In all the years I have watched her grow up it is obvious that she is quick to learn, quick to understand. And always with such boundless energy.'

'That is true,' Mrs Marshall agreed. 'In fact she is about the one child that always got on my nerves because she would never take no for an answer. Always asking questions... "What's this for, what's that for?" I have been known to give her the odd slap, I'm afraid.'

Maria Jones smiled. 'I'm sure that did her no lasting harm, Mrs Marshall.'

Presently, as they were nearing home, Mrs Marshall said, 'I do wonder how little Ruby will get on by herself when Angelina lives in at the hospital. Ruby has always depended on her, hasn't she?'

'By the sound of it,' Maria Jones said, 'little Ruby has begun to take charge of her own life. Her job is going well, and she's making other friends... no, Ruby will be all right. And anyway, I shall be keeping an eye on her from time to time, and she will be able to keep us up to date with Angelina's progress.'

They parted company, and Maria Jones said, 'I hope you find

your husband in reasonable spirits this evening, Mrs Marshall.'

'Not much chance of that,' was the laconic reply.

Maria Jones smiled to herself as she walked to her own home at the end of the terraced block of small cottages. Surprisingly, she had become quite fond of Mrs Marshall over the years, even if the woman could be difficult at times. But she worked very long hours at the orphanage to support herself and her husband, who apparently never set foot outside the door, so she probably felt tired and depressed now and again, Maria thought.

She opened her front door and went inside to the home she'd lived in most of her life, realising that she, herself, never felt depressed, even though she had lived alone for so long. She had barely known her father, and her mother had passed away when Maria was still in her teens, but she had quickly learned to be resourceful and make her own way in the world. This was mostly thanks to her mother who had taught Maria the handiwork skills that supplemented her wages as a cleaner. She regularly secured contracts from the market to make curtains and cushions and chair backs for customers, and sitting quietly by the window with her machine and needle and thread and embroidery silks, even at the end of a very long day, was her way of relaxing. They were her companions, she realised now. Her thoughts ran on, and she acknowledged that getting married had never appealed to her. Besides, just imagine having a son who might be in uniform and fighting this dreadful war! The news from the Front seemed to be getting worse every day. Imagine if someone you loved was over there…

Humming a little tune, she went into the kitchen to make a cup of tea, thinking of the two girls who'd called in to the orphanage earlier. It was lovely to see them both settled and happy with life, and Emma Kingston had looked as proud as punch to hear all their news.

And why shouldn't she be proud? She had always been as good as any blood mother to 'her' children, so any success and happiness of theirs was hers as well.

Chapter 8

December 1915

'Nurse Green! At once here, please!'

The senior nurse's imperious voice rang through the long ward, and Angelina immediately stopped folding the corners of the bed sheet she was dealing with and moved swiftly to do as she was told.

'This patient is due for his bed bath,' the senior nurse said, 'and after that please renew the dressings on his wound.'

It was the end of Angelina's second week on the men's medical ward, and even if after every shift she sometimes felt ready to fall sleep on her feet, she realised just how much she'd learned in that short time. Now, after drawing the curtains around the patient's bed, she smiled down at him.

'How are you feeling this morning?' she asked gently. She had glanced at the notes in the folder at the foot of the bed and they had stated that, among other things, the condition of 17-year-old Ralph Thomas was 'As well as might be expected'. That didn't sound very optimistic to Angelina.

'Oh, I'm all right Miss, thanks,' he said, his voice faint. 'Much better than I was this time last week, that's a fact. And it's lovely and peaceful here – quiet, not like over there.'

Angelina nodded. Young soldiers were coming in regularly now, but this was the first time she had seen one of them, and she had to admit that she was glad she hadn't been sent to the surgical ward just yet. Bathing and bandaging and general care had been her experience so far, and she was managing to satisfy her superiors that she was more than capable. But she had never seen a limb hanging off, or a scull so badly maimed that you could actually see the brain, and even though she still felt full of enthusiasm, she realised that she had a very long way to go, much to learn, hoping she didn't faint at the sight of the terrible injuries which Norma had told her about when they were together in the small bedroom they shared. Norma was older than Angelina, and had started her training at the beginning of the year. She was already waiting to be summoned to one of the theatres to assist the surgeons as they tried to put poor young men back together again.

Angelina glanced at her patient. 'Well, it's lovely that you are back in time for Christmas, isn't it?' she said. 'See – we've put up all the decorations just for you.'

He tried to smile but didn't reply. After fetching everything she needed, Angelina slipped off his hospital gown, placed protective sheeting beneath him, and very carefully removed the dressing from the large wound across his stomach, almost stepping back at the sight. The stitches were not holding, and the wound was beginning to gape and was oozing with pus.

Very, very gently, she began to wash him all over with soap and strong antiseptic.

Coughing painfully, he said, 'You look too young to be a nurse, Miss. I mean, to be doing things… things like this.'

She smiled down at him. 'Oh, I'm older than you think, and I do things like this all the time,' she said, realising that he was embarrassed. 'You just close your eyes and relax. Do you have a family?'

'My mother is still alive,' he said slowly. 'She's in South Wales where our home is.' He paused. 'I don't know if she's been told I've been sent home. Perhaps they won't bother because I'm sure I'll be going back when I'm better – it's crazy over there and men are dying like flies. They need every single one of us.'

'Oh, I'm sure your mother knows you are safe now,' Angelina said, picking up a towel and starting to smooth him dry, taking immense care around the enflamed wound. As she felt him tense under the pain, she murmured, 'Sorry, nearly done, then I'll put another dressing on this and you will feel much more comfortable.'

'I am so grateful Miss,' he said, half-closing his eyes. 'You have such a gentle, kind touch, I think you were born to be a nurse.'

'I think I was,' Angelina said softly. 'Now, you have a little nap. They will be bringing warm drinks around shortly, and I will come and check up on you later.'

Returning to the senior nurse who was sitting at her desk at the end of the ward, Angelina said, 'I have completed that – and the patient is fairly comfortable. But I'm afraid the wound is still open and the inflammation seems to be spreading.'

'Yes, I'm afraid so,' the senior nurse replied shortly. 'We will keep a close watch.' She returned her gaze to the notes in front of her. 'Now please take the temperature of the patient in bed one – it was rather high earlier, and you may need to fetch another cooling fan for him. But…' She paused. 'Thank you, Nurse Green, you are doing very well.'

Angelina was so surprised at that unexpected compliment – from a woman who seldom uttered one to any of the nurses – that she departed without replying.

The day went as every day at the hospital went. Apart from two or three lectures each week and tests being set, it was routine, routine, routine. Bed pans being constantly requested, frequent shouts and calls from patients with delirium, and nurses scurrying after consultants who arrived on the ward without notice.

When Angelina finished her twelve-hour shift at 6 p.m., having had only one short break, she admitted that she felt ready to drop. She hadn't really expected to feel this tired because fatigue was unknown to her. Perhaps, heaven forbid, she would be one of those who didn't stay the course, as the almoner had said happened to some.

Downstairs in the staff quarters she went into her room, shutting the door behind her. Then she dragged off her cap and apron and released her belt before very thankfully slipping out of her long, serge grey skirt – which felt cloying around her ankles. Then she flopped down on the bed, remembering how pleased she'd felt the first day she'd been given her uniform. She had looked at herself in the mirror with a sense of real pride, because now everyone could see that she, Angelina Green, was a real nurse.

She stared up at the ceiling defiantly. She would never give up, never! If necessary, she would die on the job!

She lay there for a few minutes, her mind still too active to doze. She wasn't feeling particularly hungry, and had only had a boiled egg and some cheese for lunch, but she'd go into the canteen in a minute for something to eat. Norma wasn't off duty until ten o'clock, so they weren't likely to see much of each other until tomorrow.

Turning her head, Angelina looked up at the coloured baubles they'd hung up, the tinsel hanging over the mirror and the door frame. Christmas decorations seemed so out of place, she thought, with that terrible war going on and young men injured and dying. Yet every ward was adorned, there were balloons everywhere, and a brightly lit Christmas tree stood guard just inside the entrance of the hospital.

Angelina's thoughts turned to her soldier... poor Ralph Thomas. Just 17, no more than a lad. He wouldn't have known that his was the first adult male body which Angelina had been asked to deal with, to touch. Of course, in the orphanage she'd seen many little boys without their clothes on, and from her

66

study books she had seen detailed pictures of fully developed male genitals, but actually coming face to face with it in all its pathetic, human vulnerability, had been something of a shock. Angelina screwed her eyes tight for a second.

And thought of Alexander.

Christmas Eve 1915

It was 10.30 a.m. – four hours into her day shift. Angelina, well wrapped up in an ungainly green apron about two sizes too big for her, and with a tight net covering her hair, was on her knees scrubbing the steel frame and legs of the bed which had held her young soldier. He had died in the night, his infected wound not responding to any medication available. He had eventually succumbed to pneumonia and now everything had to be cleaned and cleaned until not a scrap of evidence that he had been there remained. Nothing of young Ralph Thomas must be passed on.

Angelina had looked after Ralph Thomas from South Wales during his three-week stay at St Thomas's, and felt she had come to know him. She certainly liked him. He had worked on a farm, and he'd told Angelina that he was determined to own his own, one day. He'd been working with crops and animals since the age of 10, and there wasn't much he didn't know about either. He and his pal from a neighbouring farm had volunteered together to serve their country. 'It was the right thing to do,' he'd told Angelina.

Tears filled her eyes as she thought of his innocent loyalty, and she knelt back to reach for her handkerchief. Anyway, he would be in heaven now, safe, out of that horrible pain and discomfort, and hopefully surrounded by all of God's creatures that he loved so much. So she must not dwell on this, she told herself fiercely.

They had all been warned about getting too close, of feeling deeply about any of their patients, because if they did they would not be able to do the job properly. Nurses were not allowed to feel, only to work in the patient's best interests.

Dipping her scrubbing brush and cloth once more into the bucket of hot disinfectant, Angelina cleaned the last rung of the bed, wiped it all dry with a clean towel, and sat back. She'd gone over everything twice, and was satisfied that the next occupant would come to no harm.

It had taken her more than an hour to finish the job, and now she got up from her knees and picked up the bucket, aware that there were some people nearby, talking quietly.

A wave of horror swept over her as she recognised the group of visitors.

Randolph and Alexander Garfield stood there, talking to the senior nurse. Honora Mason, dressed in a beautiful red winter woollen coat and small brimmed hat, was there too, looking so pretty and demure, her tiny diamond earrings adding their lustre to her perfect appearance.

If *only* the floor could open up and swallow her, Angelina thought desperately. What must she look like, dressed like this instead of in her immaculate uniform, and looking hot and bothered and red in the face!

It was not visiting time yet, but sometimes special people were admitted out of hours, and she knew that Garfield Tobacco was a very generous patron of the hospital. So that was probably why they were here.

As she tried to sidle past the group, Alexander spoke.

'Hello, Angelina,' he said quietly, smiling down at her. 'I was hoping we might see you… Miss Kingston tells us about all of you, you know.'

'Good morning Mr Alexander,' Angelina said, hoping her voice didn't sound as strange to him as it did to her.

The senior nurse spoke up. 'Nurse Green has been standing

in for one of the cleaners this morning,' she said. 'We are a bit short-staffed because of the holiday.'

'And when do you have your holiday, Angelina?' Alexander asked. 'I hope you're not working all over Christmas!'

'No, I am on duty today and tomorrow, but I have Boxing Day off,' Angelina said, darting a glance at her superior. This was a very unusual situation, and she wished she was somewhere else – anywhere else.

'When you are cleaned up,' the senior nurse said, obviously slightly irritated at the interruption to her tour of the wards, 'please resume your normal duties here. We are expecting a new admission at two o'clock.'

Honora suddenly spoke up. 'I didn't realise that nurses had to clean the wards as well as look after patients,' she said quietly. 'You must work a very long and tiring day, Angelina.'

Angelina was surprised at the kindness of Honora Mason's tone. She had seen her several times over the years when she'd visited the orphanage with Mr Garfield and Mr Alexander, and had always thought her rather snooty and off-hand. But today she seemed genuinely interested in what Angelina was doing.

'Oh, I have only been on cleaning duty once or twice so far,' Angelina said, 'but I never mind doing it. I understood from the very beginning that nurses must be prepared to do anything required of them, whatever the circumstances.'

Honora nodded slowly. 'Well, thank goodness we have nurses,' she said. 'Who knows when any of us may need you?'

'Shall we continue your visit?' the senior nurse said, addressing Randolph. 'I believe you wish to inspect all the wards on this floor. Please follow me.'

And standing there still clutching her bucket, Angelina watched them go. As she watched, Alexander, at the end of the group, half-turned to glance back and wink at her.

'Happy Christmas, Angelina,' he mouthed silently.

Chapter 9

Boxing Day 1915

'It's so lovely to be back in my own bed,' Angelina said, glancing over at Ruby who was only just stirring. 'Sorry if I've disturbed you, Ruby – but I'm always up at this time, so my body has got used to it. I was hoping to have a lie in, but no luck. My mind thinks I'm still in uniform!'

It was still not quite six o'clock, and Ruby yawned. 'Never mind, we'll have a longer day to talk,' she said. 'I want to hear all about what you do up there, Angelina. All the gory details!'

'And I want to hear what sort of Christmas you've been having so far,' Angelina said, smiling. 'From what you've told me, you've hardly had a minute to yourself!'

Ruby sat up, hugging her knees. 'I've been thoroughly spoiled,' she said, 'because on Christmas Eve I was invited upstairs to see all the little presents they had for Nesta, and they insisted I stay there with them until quite late. Mr Carter poured us all a glass of sherry, and then we had ham rolls and mince pies.' Ruby yawned again. 'It was so kind of them and they made me feel like one of the family.'

'Did they like the presents we bought for them?' Angelina asked. Ruby nodded.

'They loved them, and there's one for each of us from them under the tree – I haven't opened mine because I thought we'd do that together today, after we've had our Boxing Day lunch.'

Angelina looked around at their little room which looked so pretty with all the decorations Ruby had bought, and with a small pile of presents tucked under the small Christmas tree with its trailing fairy lights.

'Well, considering that this is our first Christmas by ourselves, Ruby, I think you've done really well,' Angelina said. 'I wish I could have been around more to help you, but you've thought of everything.'

And it was true. Ruby had bought a small chicken for their lunch, which she'd already stuffed, the vegetables were prepared, and there were chestnuts to roast in the fire. It amazed Angelina how Ruby had come out of herself and grown up so quickly. She was so happy at work, too. It was something of a miracle, as if life in the outside world had been waiting there for Ruby Lane and she had met it head-on.

Ruby smiled happily. She had loved being in charge of things. 'And what is Christmas like at St Thomas's?'

'Oh – Christmassy,' Angelina replied. 'Well, as nice as possible, and we did have turkey for our dinner but it's very busy and we didn't have a long break. So I've been looking forward to today. But I want to hear all about you. What was Christmas Day with the Walkers like? Did it feel strange having Christmas dinner with them?'

When Ruby had told Angelina that she'd been invited there, Angelina had been doubtful. Although Ruby was not nearly as shy as she used to be, she could be anxious and unsure of herself at times, and sitting down to eat with her employers might have felt awkward.

'No, it was lovely,' Ruby said, rubbing her eyes. 'They treated

71

me as if I was a special guest. Mr Walker even pulled out my chair for me to sit down! And Robert, their son, was there too and he is really nice. He asked me everything about myself, and I told him about you, and he told me about his college and the friends he's made. He hopes to be an engineer, and I said I thought that sounded very clever and he laughed and said he would never be as clever as his parents.'

Angelina smiled. She needn't have worried about her little friend after all, because it was obvious that in the right company Ruby would always shine and be her sweet self.

'And did you have turkey with scrumptious gravy at their place?' Angelina enquired.

'Yes! And I had two helpings of everything!' Ruby said. 'Well, I didn't take much at first because I didn't want to look greedy, but Mrs Walker insisted I had more because she said I could do with some more weight on me, and Mr Walker said he thought I was just right as I was!'

'Now you're beginning to make me feel hungry, Ruby,' Angelina said, 'so I suppose we ought to start cooking the chicken – after we've had some breakfast!'

In her pyjamas, Ruby clambered out of bed and went across to the window. It was still pitch black outside, and she shivered.

'You stay there for a bit longer, Angelina,' she said, 'and I'll get the fire going. Then I'll put the oven on – we've got it to ourselves, because the Carters are out all day visiting friends.'

*

Later in the afternoon, after they'd had their dinner and opened their presents, Angelina and Ruby decided that now was the only time when they could go to the orphanage with their gifts for Miss Kingston, and chocolates for any members of the staff who were on duty.

It was cold and pouring with rain, so protected by their hooded mackintoshes, and clutching their bag of presents, the two girls started on their journey. It only took about forty minutes, but the miserable weather slowed them down as they sloshed through the puddles.

'Oh, I wish I was still going to be in my own bed tonight,' Angelina grumbled. 'One evening and one day at home are not nearly enough!'

'Never mind, I'm back at work tomorrow, too,' Ruby said. 'We open first thing in the morning as usual.'

The journey did seem to be taking a long time and Angelina said, 'Do you remember how Miss Jones sometimes got us to sing songs as we walked back from the park? Especially when we were all tired? The thing I liked most was, "This old man, he played one, he played knick-knack on my thumb, with a knick-knack, paddy-wack give a dog a bone, this old man came rolling home." Remember, Ruby?'

'Of course I do,' Ruby said. 'Miss Jones was always fun, and never ever got cross with us, did she?'

Finally, they reached the orphanage and almost at once Mrs Marshall answered their knocking with the usual resigned expression on her face.

'Happy Christmas, Mrs Marshall!' the girls chorused

'Oh, I knew that was you,' she said, standing aside for them to enter. 'Come in and take off those wet things and I'll dry them off for you.'

'It's very quiet,' Angelina said as she handed over her mackintosh. 'Where is everybody?'

'Oh well – I think the kids have worn themselves out,' Mrs Marshall said. 'You know what Christmas is like at the Garfield! Late nights and early mornings and too many toys and sweets. This afternoon Miss Kingston decided that there should be a quiet time, so they're mostly in the playroom reading or messing about with something or other.'

Angelina smiled. The festive season at the Garfield was unforgettable.

Hearing voices, Emma Kingston popped her head around her study door, and clapped her hands when she saw who it was.

'What a lovely surprise! Come in! I want to hear all your news, everything! Oh – and would you bring in tea and mince pies, Mrs Marshall, please,' she added.

Presently, after Emma Kingston had kept the girls up to date with everything going on at the Garfield, and after she had heard all about Ruby's life as a hairdresser, and what Angelina thought of St Thomas's, the three sat around the small table while the superintendent opened the presents the girls had brought for her.

There was a dainty pink scarf from Angelina, and Ruby's gift was a jar of hand cream – suggested by Mrs Walker who'd said it was the best brand she'd come across. The presents were not expensive, because neither of the girls had much money to spare, but to the superintendent they were more precious than gold.

'I shall use both of these straightaway,' she said.

'And here's a tin of Quality Street for the others,' Ruby said, reaching into her bag. 'I didn't know whether to buy peppermint creams or sugared almonds, but decided to be on the safe side because everyone likes Quality Street, don't they?' She smiled quickly. 'I am the one having to make all these important decisions, you see, because Angelina never has the time off to do any shopping. So she trusts me to try and get it right.'

'And you haven't put a foot wrong so far, Ruby,' Angelina said.

Emma Kingston marvelled, once again, at the two in front of her. These two helpless orphans, who'd come into the world with absolutely nothing, had become confident youngsters, working for their living, and obviously enjoying their freedom.

Just then there was a tap on the door and Father Laurence looked in.

'Ah – sorry to intrude,' he said, 'but the nuns were wondering when school starts again. Is it this week or next?'

'Come in, Father Laurence,' the superintendent said. 'Angelina and Ruby have called to see us. Isn't that lovely? And look – there are two mince pies left here on the plate. Would you like to take them with you?' She smiled as she spoke. The priest was very fond of his food and always seemed to know when anything sweet might be around.

Entering, he glanced down at the girls. 'It's very nice to see you both again,' he said, 'and may I wish you a most happy Christmas.' Then, after a moment, he picked up the pies and turned to go. 'Thank you, I shall enjoy these with my cup of tea,' he said.

'Oh, and by the way, Father Laurence, school won't be starting again until the week after next,' Emma Kingston said to his departing back, 'so the nuns have a nice long holiday.'

After he'd gone, the three giggled together. 'Poor man,' Emma Kingston said. 'I think he is a rather lonely soul and he does love popping in to see us.'

Angelina sighed. 'I'm afraid we shall have to go now,' she said reluctantly. 'I'm on duty first thing in the morning, so I shan't be sleeping at home tonight, worst luck.'

Ruby stood up. 'I'll go and fetch our macks from the kitchen,' she said. 'I expect Mrs Marshall has got them dry by now.'

After she'd gone, Emma Kingston looked across at Angelina kindly. 'And you really *are* enjoying the nursing world, my dear, are you?' she said. 'I mean, are you still sure that it is what you want to do? You can always change your mind, you know.'

'I never want to do anything else, Miss Kingston,' Angelina said quietly, 'and although it is very tiring and there is so much to learn and remember, and Matron's nightly round is a bit frightening – she's very, very stern – I know that this will always be the life for me.'

There was silence for a few moments, then Angelina continued, 'Mr Garfield and Mr Alexander – and Miss Honora – visited St Thomas's on Christmas Eve', Angelina said.

'Oh, did they? Well, I know Mr Garfield is a great supporter of the hospital and he always takes a genuine interest in the things he's involved with,' Emma Kingston said. 'Did they come to your ward?' Were you on duty?'

Angelina nodded. 'I'd just finished cleaning a bed in which a young soldier had just died and I was getting off my hands and knees and holding a big bucket of disinfectant. I was dressed in a horrible overall and most unbecoming hair net and smelling of carbolic and my face was all red and I must have looked an absolute fright. I mean, why couldn't I have been in my uniform? They came at just the wrong moment and I felt… awful. Especially as Miss Honora was immaculate! She was wearing the loveliest winter coat and hat and looked so pretty.' Angelina paused. 'I can't imagine what Mr Alexander thought of my appearance,' she added.

Emma Kingston's eyes softened. She leaned forward and touched Angelina's hand for a second. 'Miss Mason is certainly an attractive young lady, but shall I tell you what I think, Angelina? Mr Alexander would not even have noticed what you were wearing, or how hot and dishevelled you were looking. All he would have seen was a very beautiful young woman, doing her best.'

Chapter 10

May 1916

Angelina stirred restlessly, not wanting to wake up. It was 5 a.m., and nearly time to get ready for another long shift. While she had been deep in an exhausted sleep, how many new patients had been admitted during the night, she wondered. How many of them so injured that the ward in this hospital would be their final resting place?

Her thoughts rousing her fully, Angelina sat up, resting her head on her knees. When she had been so desperate to join the nursing profession, had she really thought about what it might entail? After all, she'd not been stupid enough to think that she would be bandaging damaged knees or putting TCP on scratches and soothing bumped heads, or wiping up sick. She had fully realised that it was going to be much more than that, but the reality of what she had seen, and had already had to deal with, had surpassed anything she might have imagined.

She smiled to herself ruefully. Perhaps it would have been better to have begun her nursing career when the country wasn't at war, because in peace-time hospitals were not likely to have seen the type of injuries that they were now confronted with every day. Then, it would have been the 'normal' trials and tribulations that beset the human body, and the treatment would have been set out neatly in all the textbooks. It would have been simple, straightforward, compared with today…

Angelina glanced over at the other bed. Norma was a theatre nurse full-time now, and there were so many injured soldiers constantly arriving that operations went on day and night. It was like a revolving door, never stopping. Norma would come off her shift and collapse down on her bed too tired to say much at all. But later, on the few opportunities when the two of them were off duty at the same time, Norma would enthrall Angelina with what had gone on, what she had assisted with. The amazing surgeons as they literally welded broken bones together, stitched back protruding internal organs, kept helpless patients alive against all the odds.

'If you've got an hour to spare,' Norma had said once, 'go to the observation balcony and watch, Angelina, if you're interested. It's fascinating.'

Was she interested? Angelina was enraptured! She had taken Norma's advice and had already stood up there several times, leaning over the balcony and taking in everything that was going on beneath her. The bright, overhead lights, the gowned and masked theatre staff moving swiftly, noiselessly, to obey the surgeon's terse request for the specific, sterile instrument he needed at that vital moment. Angelina had watched, fascinated. This wasn't just medicine, it was magic!

And perhaps, one day, she, too, might join that illustrious group of the medical profession – the surgeons! She might become one of them, if she was determined…

Now, she took a deep breath, trying to stem the kaleidoscope of thoughts that constantly filled her brain. For the moment, she was doing all right, passing all the tests without difficulty, though lectures had become less frequent because every nurse was needed on duty, and quite often it was a case of learning as they went along, learning on the job.

*

Later on, Angelina had just finished her fourth bed bath for the day when she felt a tug on her arm. She turned quickly. It was the new young nurse who'd only just come onto the ward and who was looking frightened.

'Could you come over here a minute and help me?' she whispered, darting an anxious glance in the direction of the senior nurse who had her back to them at the far end of the ward. 'I should know what to do, but I'm afraid I don't, and I'm feeling a bit funny.'

'Don't worry,' Angelina said softly, accompanying her to the patient five beds along. 'What's happening?'

'He's gurgling and making such a funny noise, and he looks terrible…'

They approached the patient and Angelina gasped inwardly as she saw the problem. Quickly, she reached for a bed pan just in time to catch the flow of blood coming from his mouth and lungs, and she supported him firmly as he leaned over.

'Hold on, we'll soon put you right,' she said briskly. 'All this will be over in a minute. Take short breaths when you are able to. That's it… try and keep calm.'

As she stood there trying to reassure him, Angelina felt her knees shaking. This was a typical symptom of advanced tuberculosis which she'd read about many times, but she'd never seen blood in this quantity oozing and bubbling from a patient. It was a horrible sight, and the poor man was coughing painfully, trying to clear his airways.

'Don't worry, you'll soon be all right again,' she said. Then she glanced at the other girl who was as white as a sheet. 'Fetch some warm water and disinfectant so we can clean this up and make him more comfortable,' Angelina said quietly, but the words were barely out of her mouth before the young nurse slipped to the floor in a dead faint, just as the senior nurse arrived on the scene, her eyebrows raised. It was unusual for any member of staff to collapse while on duty.

'Oh dear,' she said casually. 'Thank you, Nurse Green, I will see to this patient while you revive your colleague.'

*

'It wasn't very nice, Ruby,' Angelina said, next time they were together. 'I felt so sorry for the other girl. When she came round she was inconsolable, saying that they'd never let her go on training. But it was only her second day on the ward and she hadn't got used to any of it.' Angelina made a face. 'We never know what each day is going to bring.'

Ruby shuddered. 'I honestly don't know how you do any of it,' she said. 'I mean, the worst that can happen to me is that I don't satisfy a client that I've got her set right or that I've let water run down the back of her neck and soaked her clothes! And so far, thank goodness I've been proved not guilty of either!'

It was a Friday and one of Angelina's rare days off. As they sat at home in their little room she was telling Ruby about what had happened earlier in the week.

'I think it's really kind of Mrs Walker to let you have today off so we can spend it together,' Angelina said, as they sipped their morning coffee. 'From all you say, she seems a wonderful person to work for – you really are happy, aren't you, Ruby? You don't some-times wish you were doing something else, or somewhere else?'

'Never,' Ruby said at once. 'It's funny, but I never gave a thought about what I would do when I left the Garfield. Of course, I always knew that Miss Kingston would make sure I was all right, and as long as I was still with you, Angelina, I didn't worry about a thing.'

'Well, unfortunately we're not together all that much now, are we?' Angelina said. 'But it doesn't matter because you are quite happy being here by yourself most of the time, aren't you?'

Ruby thought about that for a moment. 'I'm actually not alone all that much,' she said, 'because Mrs Carter is always popping down to see me, and I do look after Nesta for them whenever they want me to.' Ruby smiled happily. 'The baby is growing into the sweetest little thing you ever saw, and I often go up there to help at bath time.'

'I'd quite like to work on the children's ward one day,' Angelina said thoughtfully. 'It would be a change and something of a relief! But as far as I can see, I'm rooted to my particular spot at the moment.'

'And the other thing is, as I've mentioned before,' Ruby went on, 'Mrs Walker regularly invites me to have Sunday dinner with them. I sometimes make an excuse and don't go because I don't want her to feel she has to ask me.' Ruby paused. 'I suppose I'm a bit of extra company because I think they really miss their son when it's just the two of them there at home.'

Angelina nodded. Ruby's life really had knitted up together, and that was largely thanks to Miss Kingston who seemed to have an instinct about what was right for her orphans. It didn't work every time, but it did more often than not.

'Do you realise we've been working girls for more than a year, now,' Ruby said. 'When I started at the shop I never thought that I would be doing sets and perms. Something I haven't told you, Angelina, is that last month Mrs Walker started training me to do cutting! She has a list of young customers who come in and are prepared to risk their styling in my hands so I can practise – they get a free shampoo and set as a reward, and of course she watches me like a hawk! I wouldn't dare snip in the wrong place!' Ruby smiled. 'Although I really shake when I begin, I'm not doing badly. Mrs Walker says she is really pleased with my progress.' Ruby sat back and finished the last of her coffee. 'So there you are, Angelina, I love my job – but are you as happy as I am? Honestly? Would you like to be doing something else? You know, when it's been a bad day and you're really tired?'

There was a long pause before Angelina replied. 'I have some-thing to tell you, Ruby,' she said, and Ruby looked up, startled. Surely Angelina wasn't going to say that she wanted to change her mind and not be a nurse after all? After everything she'd always said? That would be a tremendous turnaround!

'I honestly believe that when I came into the world – whenever and wherever that was,' Angelina went on slowly, 'my destiny had already been decided for me. All I want to do for the rest of my life is to care for sick people, and to get better and better at it… to become a senior nurse… or even a matron one day. And as I go on learning, to push my knowledge and experience to the furthest limit.' She smiled briefly. 'And whatever horrible thing life throws at me in the future, I'll lob it straight back. Nothing will ever make me desert my post.'

'Well then, that's us two sorted,' Ruby said. 'Everything in the garden's lovely – at least for the time being!' She stood to pick up their coffee cups. 'Come on – shall we go into town for a change and hit the shops? I've had so many tips lately my purse is quite full, so I can buy us afternoon tea and cakes later.'

*

At the end of the month as usual, the senior nurse knocked on Matron's door and went in. This regular meeting was held to discuss staff in general – which of them may not be giving satis-faction or any who were to be switched to another ward. But for the last year, the essential focus had been on which nurse could be spared to join the medical staff in France. The situation, Matron had been informed, was becoming so desperate it was essential for more and more nurses to be transferred.

'Ah, good – come in, nurse,' Matron said. 'What do you have for me this month?'

The senior nurse put her file down on the desk. 'Not too much to report, Matron,' she said. 'Very few call in sick or come in late for their shift. In factm I have a fairly good team at the moment.' She paused. 'One trainee had a bit of difficulty at the beginning of the month – but she's getting much better at the sight of blood. I told her we all had to go through that.'

Matron smiled briefly. 'Well then, she will obviously not be one of the nurses I am going to ask you to shortly release for war duty.' She glanced up. 'In your opinion, are there any who are ready and capable to join the fray? I am told that they would like the next batch at the beginning of August, which is when medical staff who have been over there for a while are due to be sent home for some respite.'

The senior nurse sighed. 'I've only got one who really stands out, I'm afraid,' she said, 'and I would recommend her with regret because she would be greatly missed on the ward. She has become very competent, reacting to any situation with a calm and courage that belies her youth and experience.'

'Of course the perfect candidate, then,' Matron said. 'Am I to assume you are referring to Angelina Green?'

'I am,' the senior nurse said slowly.

'So, you have two months to try and prepare Nurse Green for what lies ahead of her,' Matron said. 'I have been asked to release six altogether,' she added, 'so wish me luck that I can produce another five of equal calibre.'

Chapter 11

As soon as she had her next day off, Angelina went straight to the orphanage with her great news. She was going to war!

As usual, the front door was opened by Mrs Marshall. 'Goodness me, have you run all the way here?' she asked. 'You look quite hot and bothered.'

'Hello Mrs Marshall – is it possible for me to see Miss Kingston?' Angelina said. 'I won't keep her long because I'm back on night duty at six.'

'She is here, having her afternoon cup of tea,' Mrs Marshall said, leading Angelina long the corridor towards the superintendent's study. 'Miss Jones is here as well. I'm sure they will both be pleased that you've called in.'

At that moment, the study door opened and Maria Jones emerged, a file under her arm. Her eyes lit up when she saw Angelina.

'Angelina! How lovely to see you!' she exclaimed. She turned back briefly. 'Miss Kingston, guess who's here!'

The superintendent immediately joined the small group, and automatically gave Angelina a brief hug. 'Well, this calls for another pot of tea,' she said. 'Would you mind, Mrs Marshall?'

Nodding, Mrs Marshall departed, while the other three went back into the superintendent's study and sat down.

'Now, I have a funny feeling that you've got something special to tell us, Angelina,' Emma Kingston said. 'Let me guess… you've become Matron at St Thomas's! I knew it wouldn't take you long!'

Angelina smiled broadly. 'I know you've always had great faith in me, Miss Kingston,' she said, 'but no, I'm not Matron yet.' She took a deep breath. 'What I've come to tell you is that I am being sent to France to nurse the wounded, and I can't wait because I've never been anywhere but England – as you know, Miss Kingston – and although I'm a bit frightened, I'm also really excited! It will be a whole new world for me, something I never expected!'

Emma Kingston looked thoughtful for a moment. 'When do you go, Angelina?' she asked.

'Well, at first they told us to be prepared to leave in August,' Angelina said, 'but apparently the war is so terrible that plans have been pushed forward and now we are to leave at the very end of June – in just a couple of weeks! I hope I remember to pack everything I may need over there,' she added.

Emma Kingston smiled inwardly. Angelina Green wouldn't forget a single thing. 'How many of you are to go?' the superintendent asked soberly. 'I take it there are to be a number of you?'

'Yes, six of us are going from St Thomas's,' Angelina replied. 'I didn't know any of them before, but we've had a group meeting and the others seem really nice. I was the only one selected from my ward.'

'And have you been given any idea exactly where you are going, or what you may find when you get there?' the superintendent asked quietly.

'Not really,' Angelina said. 'We know we're going to France to one of the battlefield hospitals, and that there will be large numbers of wounded soldiers arriving all the time. But it will all become clear when we actually get there. Patching up bleeding wounds won't be too much bother for me because the medical ward I've been working on for months has been very good experience.'

Maria Jones had not spoken a word as she absorbed all that Angelina was saying. Now, she said, 'And how does Ruby feel about this? I imagine she is a bit upset that you are leaving, isn't she?'

Angelina shook her head quickly. 'No, Ruby wishes she was coming too and is nearly as excited as I am! Fancy going to a foreign country! I expect this will be my only chance to travel – and of course, I am sorry that it's because of the war, but it will be a huge experience which I will take with me for the rest of my life! Fortunately, when our landlord heard I would not be living at home for a bit, and the reason for it, he said it didn't matter about my rent not being paid for a while, that there were more important things to consider when there was a war on.' Angelina finished the last of her tea before adding, 'Anyway, Ruby has been given quite a big pay rise, and she's not worried at all about handling everything without me there.'

Angelina stood up to leave. 'I'd better go,' she said. 'I won't bother to return home for a meal, I'll have something in the canteen. Then I'm on a twelve-hour shift – so wish me a quiet night!'

Emma Kingston felt pride bubbling up in her chest. What a long way this little scrap had come in her life.

'Promise that you'll write and tell us how you are, and how you are getting on over there, Angelina,' the superintendent said, standing to give her another hug.

'Of course I will write to you. And anyway, I don't expect I'll be gone all that long.'

Maria Jones moved over and took both Angelina's hands in her own. 'Promise that you will take great care of yourself, my dear, won't you?' she said softly. 'And don't worry about little Ruby. I will make sure she doesn't feel neglected.'

It was with some surprise that Angelina saw tears well up in Maria Jones's eyes. Not much of that kind of emotion went on at the Garfield, but Miss Jones had always been a bit different from any of the others. She was always kind and full of sympathy even over minor mishaps any of the orphans experienced, while Miss Kingston, though never anything but gentle, was more business-like and pragmatic. After all, she had been in sole charge of an orphanage for a very long time. She could not afford to weep too many tears, and certainly not in public.

Angelina squeezed Maria Jones's hand in return. 'Of course I will take great care of myself, Miss Jones,' she said. 'Don't worry, I don't think I will be expected to handle a gun or anything too dangerous! I'll be well away from the fight! And thank you very much for offering to keep an eye on Ruby.' Angelina smiled. Ruby had always been a special favourite of Maria Jones.

Saturday 1st July, 1916

'Oh, I feel ghastly! I want to go back... I want to go home! I hope I'm given a nice comfy bed to recover on.'

Angelina glanced at her new friend, Heather, as they got off the boat which had just brought them over the channel. It had been rather a choppy crossing and several of the nurses had been sick. 'Cheer up,' Angelina said, 'I'm sure there's a nice cup of tea waiting for us.'

'I'd rather settle for a glass of champagne,' said Jane, the other friend Angelina had palled up with. 'I wonder if they'll throw a cocktail party to greet us.'

Angelina looked at her briefly. Of course Jane was joking, but of all the nurses, she was the one who stood out as very rich, and rather posh, sometimes giving the impression that she was far superior to anyone else. Apparently, she lived with her parents in a big house in Surrey and had always gone to a private school. So champagne and cocktail parties would be commonplace for her, Angelina thought. Jane had never bothered to enquire about Heather or Angelina's background, the few chats they'd had together so far being all about Jane. Well, Angelina thought, whatever had happened to any of them in the past, for the foreseeable future they were all to be in exactly the same boat and she hoped Jane realised what she'd done in agreeing to do war service after just a few months' training.

'It was so *boring* at home,' Jane had said once on the boat. 'There was never anything to do, so on a whim I started at St Thomas's.'

Now, the small group made their way towards the line of trucks waiting to drive the latest contingent of relief workers to the field hospital, and Angelina looked up at the soldier escorting them

'Am I hearing thunder or is that guns?' she asked innocently.

'That, Miss, is bombardment,' the man said cheerfully. 'There's a terrible "how do ye do" going on at the moment – has been for days; guns and guns and more guns. Theirs and ours. They're not very far off and it's noisy, innit? We'll all be stone deaf at the end of this lot. But don't worry, you'll get used to it, you'll get used to the whole damn thing.'

For the first time since she'd been told she was to go to the war zone, Angelina felt a shiver of panic run down her spine. Although they had been given some details about the situation they would find themselves in, she hadn't allowed herself to dwell on it. She'd dwelt on the glorious fact that she had been one of the chosen ones to go over and do her bit and it had made her feel important, special. She'd focused on all the details concerning her departure from England – what to take, what to leave behind, last minute goodbyes to friends and colleagues. But now they were here, walking on French soil. And, within a few hours, if what they'd been told was true, she and the others would be seeing things only the devil could have devised.

It was a long drive to their destination, and to the wooden huts which were the nurses' living quarters. Their room had six camp beds, and Jane was the first to collapse down onto one of them.

'Oh deary me,' she said. 'No springs on this, I'm afraid, and a *very* coarse blanket! But thank God we're stationary at last. Where's that cup of tea you mentioned, Angelina?'

Presently, with Red Cross ambulances coming and going, and with the constant, thunderous boom of not so distant guns in their ears, the girls were shown to the field canteen. After a meal of bread and ham and beetroot, and the much longed for mugs of tea, they were taken to the hospital where they'd be working until at least Christmas, so they'd been told. As they approached, Angelina's eyes widened.

The hospital was a long, brown, tented construction, much bigger than she'd imagined it would be, with the Union Jack fluttering defiantly above the entrance. And as they entered, a young doctor came forward.

'Greetings, and welcome to hell,' he said, giving them a crooked smile. 'Needless to say, we are very thankful to have you here. My name is Dr Lewis – you can call me Sam – and you are…?'

The girls each gave their names, and Dr Lewis promptly said, 'I won't remember any of that, of course, so all you'll hear is me regularly yelling for a nurse. So be prepared! Unfortunately for you, the war has been at full height for many days and shows no sign of stalling. In fact, the expected advance is now in progress, which means that casualties will be coming in, in waves. We expect another train load any time.' He shrugged wearily. 'The only advice I can give you is to use your skills whenever and wherever you see the need. That's how it works. But there are several doctors here on and off, so don't be afraid to ask. The operating theatre is the tent behind this one – you will be needed there from time to time.'

Before he could say any more Angelina put up her hand.

'Excuse me,' she said, feeling slightly silly to be asking a simple question, 'but where exactly are we? I mean, I know we're some-where in France, but…'

Well, how was she expected to know? She had never been

anywhere but London in her life before, and any details they'd been given about their whereabouts had been sparse.

Dr Lewis paused briefly. 'Roughly speaking, we're close to the valley of the Somme,' he said, 'and while I believe it is an enchanting place under normal circumstances, I personally do not want to get any nearer to it than we are at the moment. In other words, Nurse Green, we are all in the front line of this cursed affair.'

He smiled kindly at her, and she was surprised that he'd remembered her name. She would not have known that, of the six new recruits, it had been her open gaze and bright, interested expression that he'd noticed as they'd introduced themselves. It had looked to him, even during those few seconds, that this young nurse was ready to get involved straightaway, like a child at sports day waiting for the signal to start running the race.

'So now you know where you are, let me give you a short tour of the wards,' Dr Lewis said. 'Follow me.'

Angelina liked Dr Lewis. He'd held nothing back and was the sort of person you could trust. He wasn't very old, she thought, probably in his twenties, but he looked tired, and held an air of resignation.

The six nurses followed obediently behind him, through another flapped doorway and along towards the main entrance to the wards.

At first sight, Angelina thought she was in the middle of a terrible nightmare as moans and groans and shouting and cursing met their ears. There seemed to be one long ward which went on and on for miles, and which was sectioned off in various places by screens. And along each side were rows and rows of beds, all close together, every one of them occupied. The nurses on duty barely looked up at the visitors, though a couple did give a brief wave of the hand.

'Sorry it's a bit noisy,' Dr Lewis said, glancing at the girls. 'A lot of it's thanks to shellshock and gassing – but you'll get used to the din.' He paused. 'We do our best,' he said quietly, 'and sometimes our best is good enough.'

Angelina swallowed hard. It was true that occasionally they'd had some delirious patients on the medical ward at St Thomas's, but nothing like this! This was like being in a mental asylum – but these patients were not mad, they were soldiers who'd been fit men before they joined up. And now they were helpless and pathetic, some calling for their mothers over and over again. It was heartbreaking to listen to, and Angelina wanted to cover her ears. But she stopped herself. She was a nurse, here to do her duty, and she would never show any sign of weakness – never!

Well, she would try not to…

They followed the doctor through to each ward as he explained everything to them – the section for the medical cases, the one for patients awaiting surgery, those who were on the point of death – and despite all her good intentions, Angelina admitted that it was almost too much to take in. Where on earth did you start in such places? The only wards she'd known were kept strictly clean – and she should know because she'd had more than one turn at scrubbing beds and floors and lavatories, 'No death by infection here!' the senior nurse had often declared. But this hospital in France looked anything but clean to Angelina. How could it be, with blood staining every sheet, every bandaged head wet and oozing pus, with dazed patients suddenly sitting up and trying to grab at their dressings, coughing and spitting? How could you possibly ensure hygiene in these circumstances? And the smell… the smell was like nothing Angelina had ever experienced.

At last, they got to the end of the wards, and Dr Lewis said casually, 'The operating theatre is here at the end, and across the road is the mortuary. Full up at the moment, as it happens. We're waiting for the burial crew to arrive because more mortuary space will undoubtedly be needed in the next day or so.'

As they'd been walking through the wards one or two of the nurses had asked simple questions relating to where any equipment they might need was stored, but Jane wanted to know something else.

'How long are our shifts likely to be, Dr Lewis?'

He shrugged. 'As long as we need you, I'm afraid,' he said simply. 'But don't worry too much about that. You will be given time off, of course, but for obvious reasons that's bound to be patchy.' He glanced at his watch. 'What I do suggest is that you all get a good night's sleep so that you can report here in the morning at six o'clock to take over from the nurses you are replacing. They are going home tomorrow, lucky things.'

Chapter 12

Angelina hardly slept a wink that night. The sights and sounds of those wards had ground themselves into her brain with such intensity that she had to creep outside to the latrines to be sick. But she wasn't sick. She just waited there for several minutes, taking deep breaths until the horrible feeling had passed.

She pressed her lips together tightly, cross with herself. They hadn't even begun their mission, yet, so she could hardly afford to fall at the first fence. Imagine being sent home as unfit for duty! That thought was enough, and Angelina was never again to experience the slightest form of any illness while in France.

The night was dark, and it was starting to rain again as she began to make her way back to the hut, almost bumping into Heather who was on her own way to the toilets.

'Couldn't you sleep either?' Heather said quietly. 'I've been tossing and turning, and those beds! They're like rocks!'

Angelina agreed, smiling. 'When we get back home, the ones at St Thomas's will make us feel we're sleeping on gossamer.' She nodded briefly towards their hut. 'None of the others seem to be having any trouble sleeping,' she said.

'Especially not Jane!' Heather said. 'She's right next to me and she's been snoring all night!'

'Yes, I've been listening to her,' Angelina said. 'We were all too tired to talk much last night, but did you really expect to see such appalling things, Heather? Such appalling injuries? I have to admit, it shook me a bit. I couldn't help wondering if I should have been chosen to come over here at all. What possible use can I be to those men? Most of them are in the worst state you could ever imagine, aren't they?'

Heather nodded. 'I'm with you there, Angelina,' she said, 'but my father served as a medical officer in the Boer war, and when he knew I was coming over he told me that I mustn't think of the dreadful things I may see as being suffered by real men. He said that I should think of it as handling models to be practised on. And that you must shut your ears to any noise they're making and get the job done as quickly and painlessly as possible.'

Angelina turned to go, pulling her coat more closely around her. 'Thanks for sharing that advice, Heather,' she said. 'I'll see if it works for me.'

Four days later...

At six o'clock Angelina and the others trudged through the wet grass towards the hospital, ready to start their morning shift. Every single thing they had been trained to do had swung into action, and it had surprised them all how soon they'd felt able to touch and handle their patients and deal with the grotesque necessities required by severely damaged bodies and minds, and how they managed to go on calmly throughout the din and disruption.

It helped that some of the men even had the heart to have a laugh. This morning, as they began their individual duties, Jane, especially, seemed to have been picked out for some teasing.

'Come to the pub with me tonight, Miss,' one of them said. 'I'd like the chance to get *you* drunk!'

Jane grinned affably. 'Don't kid yourself,' she said. 'I could drink you under the table any day!!'

Those who could join in the banter managed to smile, then Jane said to the first man, 'Now then, clever sticks, I'm about to remove this dressing. It'll take a minute or two and it's going to hurt like hell. But you're a big strong lad and you're not going to make a fuss, are you?'

'I'm gonna tell my mum about you,' the man said. 'She'll have a word or two to say that'll pin your ears back!'

With everything she needed in front of her, Jane leaned over, biting her lip at what she had to do. It was a terrible wound, the intestines protruding, and the area severely infected. Then she smiled quickly. 'Tell you what,' she said, 'Who knows "Ten Green Bottles"?'

And with that several voices began joining in feebly. 'Hanging on the wall...'

'Good! Now everyone sing as loud as you can until we get to, let's see... six green bottles. Okay? That should be long enough to get this done.'

Obediently, several soldiers began the familiar song, and Angelina, working three beds along, began humming along too. She remembered that that was another of Miss Jones's favourites. Amazingly, by the time the wound was cleaned and re-dressed, half the ward was singing.

Angelina glanced across at Jane and winked. That was clever of Jane.

But a moment or two later, her patient sank back in a state of collapse. He had managed to sing to the end with the others, but that was the last sound he would ever make. He became deeply unconscious and never recovered.

The following day, as the girls rounded the corner to the hospital, each one of them stopped short, the sight almost freezing the blood in their veins.

What they were looking at were hundreds and hundreds of stretchers being carried towards them, everyone and everything covered in thick brown mud. Some of the wounded were managing to stagger and crawl along, cursing and calling out for help. It was the most pitiful and frightening thing to see, and Angelina's first thought was – how on earth are we going to treat all these men and where are we going to put them? There was hardly any space left on the wards and there were so many wounded you could barely count them.

She moved forward quickly, gritting her teeth. This wasn't the time for thinking, this was the time for action, and all the nurses, together with other medical staff who had emerged from the hospital, automatically took up position as they went from stretcher to stretcher, and from one walking wounded to another, assessing which needed immediate attention, which could await their turn.

Angelina swiftly moved along the line. No amount of book learning, no amount of technical description could cover this event. You had to be here to witness this unbelievable scene, to hear the desperate cries and delirious moans.

The plight of one soldier almost took her breath away. He was reaching out to take hold of anyone who might pass by. 'Help, someone please,' he called, and Angelina, horror-stricken at his plight, went straight to him, and he clutched her hand.

'Sorry to be a nuisance,' he said through parched lips, 'but I can't see anything, anything at all. Will I have to have an operation? I'm only 17,' he added, 'and I've never been to hospital.'

Angelina squeezed his hand in both of hers. 'Don't you worry about a thing,' she said. 'You are safe now, and we're going to make you comfortable. You'll soon be going home.'

Her voice trembled as she spoke. Both his eyes had been shot through, the top of his face a mangled mess of blood and mud.

This young soldier would never see anything again. Not in this world.

That summer month, more usually known for beach holidays and basking in the sun, would be remembered by Angelina as an endless nightmare. As each day was succeeded by another exactly like it, time seemed to stay still and hang suspended, waiting for some conclusion, some relief, some release.

Her duties, as with everyone else on the nursing staff, became rhythmical, from the mundane and methodical to the extraordinary and unbelievable. It became quite normal for Angelina to work part of most days in the operating theatre, and what she was seeing both fascinated and shocked her. Going from having merely watched the procedures at St Thomas's to actually assisting the surgeons as they amputated limbs or bored through skulls, was a gigantic step. Yet she admitted that she preferred being in the operating theatre than working on the wards. For one thing, the patient was usually quiet and still – though that was not always the case as anaesthetic was sometimes in short supply – and to observe the skill of the surgeons as they sawed into a body or screwed joints and bones back in place, never failed to amaze Angelina. Although she had never been a theatre nurse at home, she remembered enough of what she had seen and read about that she could react to everything demanded of her without hesitation. She knew the names of all the instruments by heart, and knew what each one was for. When they were called for, they were in the surgeon's hands within a second. All of which meant that barely a day passed without Nurse Green being requested for urgent theatre duty.

The days and weeks passed by relentlessly, with more soldiers arriving all the time, and by now the injuries of the wounded had become familiar, Put simply, it was a case of attempting to keep smashed bodies alive by whichever means were available, and it had to be admitted that although seeing such terrible injuries was always grossly disturbing, all the nurses had become able to treat the wounded as Heather's father had once advised. Think with your head, not with your heart. This is all pretend. While that could have appeared heartless, it was the only way, and it got the job done.

Even more difficult to deal with was the continuous stream of soldiers coming in with shellshock. At first it was hard to take in. Grown men, young men, not horribly wounded in the body but desperately ill in the mind. Gibbering and muttering, shouting out swear words which Angelina had never heard in her life before. Calling out for their mates who'd been killed. Going over and over what they'd seen, what they'd been through. This condition, though unusual to some of the nurses, was vaguely recognised by Angelina. Because hadn't little Ruby gone through her own form of shellshock when she'd been no more than a baby? Hadn't Ruby been subjected to terrible sounds, terrible hurts, which had left her unable to talk for the first few years of her life? And at first, when she did speak, it was usually gabbling and stuttering, accompanied by throwing herself against the wall in a frenzy. And hadn't she, Angelina, instinctively known how to help? By listening to her, talking quietly, distracting the damaged mind with simpler, happier thoughts and diversions. It had taken time, but Ruby had recovered.

Angelina sighed deeply. Perhaps some of these poor men were so far gone that there'd be no cure for them, but others would get better if they were patient, and in the right hands. Until then, she would console them as best she could. She would tell them to hold on and think of the moment they would all be back home enjoying that first pint of bitter in an English pub.

The following weeks proved more arduous than ever, with more and more casualties coming in each day, and one morning the nurses were woken at 4 a.m. to deal with a convoy of wounded who'd just arrived. There appeared to be only about fifteen who were able to walk, the rest were on stretchers, and Angelina, with Jane right beside her, walked quickly forward.

'Whatever can we do with this one, Jane?' Angelina murmured

as they reached a stretcher holding a soldier with his chest shot through, his intestines sticking out through his ribs. But at almost the same moment, the young lad said cheerfully, 'Well, what do you know! Two gorgeous girls have come to my rescue!'

Angelina gasped inwardly. How could anyone with such injuries even talk, never mind make a joke! As usual, Jane chipped in.

'We've been waiting for you, soldier,' she said heartily. 'What kept you?'

He managed a grin. 'Bloody Germans, that's what, Miss,' he said. Then his expression crumbled, and he groaned, 'I hope you've got some of the hard stuff on hand – I could down a whole damn bottle all to myself.'

'Coming up!' Jane said. 'With some ice and lemon, of course! Now, you lie still and we'll get you into the ward.' She beckoned to one of the orderlies to take the stretcher.

Angelina said quietly, 'Isn't it amazing that they can keep so cheerful, with all they're going through?' She shook her head slowly.

Jane replied, 'Isn't what we're doing, Angelina? Isn't that the only way we get through anything that ruddy life throws at us? All the ups and downs?'

Angelina didn't reply to that, but wondered what Jane had meant because from everything she had said about her past had suggested that she'd been born with a silver spoon in her mouth, with everything going her way. She had never thought to ask Angelina about her past.

The nurses went on from one stretcher to another, and as Angelina approached one at the far end of the row, the soldier called out, 'Danke, Miss, danke…?'

'Danke?' That was a German, a German prisoner lying helplessly and begging for assistance. Angelina's first, fleeting thought was – this is an enemy soldier who's been wounding and killing our own men. How can I possibly care for him. How can I possibly care *about* him?

But before those thoughts were even a second old, Angelina had gone straight over to him. This was not a vile German enemy but a sick human being, a young man forced into conflict, far away from hearth and home, and he was terribly wounded. Both his arms appeared completely useless and the dressing on his head was seeping blood and pus. She smiled down at him and murmured the only two words she knew in German.

'Guten Morgen,' she said quietly. 'Good morning.' And she was rewarded by a pathetically grateful smile. She touched his cheek gently. 'We are going to the hospital.' He smiled again. 'To make you better,' she said. 'And one day you will be going back home.'

As she watched him eventually being taken to the ward, Angelina realised that he was the only German she had ever met face to face. In fact, the only foreigner from any country. She had been brought up in the caring, secluded environment of the Garfield orphanage, and although she knew that Miss Kingston would never have turned any child away, whatever colour or creed, Angelina had only ever met English people.

Suddenly, amongst all this mud and mayhem, all the swearing and cries of distress, Angelina thought of home. As soon as she came off duty, she would write to Miss Kingston.

But it was another three weeks before she was off duty for long enough to sit down with her pen and paper.

It was quite late at night, others alongside her in an exhausted sleep or two still on the wards, and propping herself up on her pillow, Angelina began, remembering what they'd been told. All letters would be read and vetted before posting, and no details of their whereabouts or what they were doing were to be revealed.

Dear Miss Kingston

This is the first moment that I have been able to actually sit down and write to you, and I'm sorry for the delay. But we are kept so busy that by the time our shift has ended all we do is flop down on our beds and go to sleep. Two of the nurses in the hut are here now, out for the count!

I am only allowed to tell you that I am using my nursing abilities to the full and so far, I am managing all right, learning a lot as I go along. The friends sharing our hut are all very nice and we have become quite close – probably because most of us are having to deal with medical cases we'd never have thought to experience, and it's a comfort to talk to each other about our feelings. But we manage to have a laugh now and again, and the food is pretty good. Not like Mrs Haines's, I must admit, but we get so hungry that quantity rather than quality is the first expectation!

I have no idea when I might be allowed home for a rest – it hasn't even been mentioned – but we do get time off now and again and it's not too long a walk to some small shops. Not that any of us feel like shopping, but it's a relief to think of other things just for a little while.

I think of all of you such a lot and hope all is well. Give my love to everyone (including Mrs Marshall!) and especially to Miss Jones who I know is taking care of Ruby for me – not that I think Ruby needs much taking care of, but it's still nice to think of that. And should you see them, please give my regards to Mr Randolph and Mr Alexander.

Please don't worry about me, Miss Kingston. I am taking great care not to become ill or do something silly, which would make my presence here worthless. But I am not afraid to say that despite all I see and do here, I am happy. That's strange, isn't it? But you know, better than anyone, how much I've always wanted to grow up quickly and do what I'm doing now. One day, I will be able to tell you all about it, but that will have to wait because this terrible war shows no sign of abating.

Good night, Miss Kingston. I send you my best love, now and always.

Angelina.

101

As she sealed down and stamped her letter, Angelina sighed briefly. What she would like to have added — because it would have helped to ease the sorrow in her heart — was that tomorrow, she was to assist at the operation on the young German who was having both his arms amputated.

Chapter 13

18th November 1916

Autumn came early that year, accompanied by endless rain, which meant that the hundreds upon hundreds of wounded soldiers arriving were always plastered from head to foot in thick brown mud, their life blood mixed up with the filth.

The very worst thing for Angelina was seeing the rows and rows of dead piled up in the mortuary which was always full to overflowing. There was little time or opportunity for much dignity, and each body was merely covered by a single blanket, and with bare feet sticking out. To her, that was the saddest sight because these soldiers were now beyond her help – she was useless to them. There was no more chance to relieve their suffering, and it felt like a personal failure, as if Nurse Green hadn't got to them quickly enough.

But Angelina soon managed to quell her morbidity because she knew such thoughts were silly. She worked tirelessly all day, and many nights with little time off, and would go on doing so until she dropped. She was 16 years old... 16? Time, and the experiences which had gone with it, had made her grow up very quickly, and inside, she felt that she was at least 60!

Early one morning, Dr Lewis sent word to all the nursing staff that that they should report to him immediately, and Angelina and the others quickly got into their uniforms. What now, they wondered.

They, and other nurses, arrived at the doctor's office which was the small tent at the entrance to the hospital where they had received their first instructions. How long ago that seemed now, Angelina thought. Dr Lewis came straight to the point.

'We have been informed that fighting this particular battle has now ceased,' he said, his voice expressionless. 'Of course, it does not mean that we shan't be receiving any more casualties – far from it, because there'll be a massive backlog, but—'

Angelina couldn't hold back. 'I'm sorry, do you mean the war is *over*?' she said incredulously. And for the first time that morning she suddenly realised that the relentless booming of guns had stopped, making it feel comparatively peaceful. That hideous din had become so much the norm, she hadn't even noticed it was no longer there.

'No, I'm afraid the war is certainly not over, Nurse Green,' the doctor said, 'but the battle of the Somme has been halted because it has reached an impasse, and apparently it is thought a stand-off is the more sensible decision.'

There was a stunned silence as they all took in this news, then Jane said, 'So all the men who have lost their limbs and their lives have done so for absolutely nothing? That this… this ghastly bloody mayhem has been a complete waste of time?' Her voice trembled with emotion and there was a general murmur of agreement at her words. A fight that nobody won? How could that possibly be?

Dr Lewis shrugged. 'It must look like that,' he said slowly, 'but presumably lessons have been learned along the way so that future plans are better formulated and the same mistakes not repeated.'

Angelina looked at him quickly. She could see that he, too, was deeply upset at this unexpected turnaround of events. All the blood which had been spilt, the countless lives damaged beyond repair...

All because the war lords sitting comfortably in their offices had got it wrong.

The doctor turned briskly. 'Right, well now you know as much as I do,' he said, 'and our work will continue as normal for many weeks. Casualties will be coming over until the battlefield has been cleared, and this will probably take some time.' Dr Lewis allowed himself a brief smile. 'So I don't want any of you to feel that you are no longer essential here, because you are.' He hesitated for a second. 'And this might be a good moment to thank you all for the sterling work you have put in from the moment you arrived. I, and the other doctors, could not have managed without a single one of you.' He smiled again. 'Of course, that was only interim praise because you are certain to deserve much more of it before the end of all this. I'm afraid the war hasn't finished with you, or with any of us, yet,' he added.

Heather suddenly spoke. 'When things have quietened here,' she said, 'will we be sent elsewhere?'

The doctor nodded. 'Yes, though we haven't been told much yet. But it's obvious that fighting is still going on all along the Front, so it's likely that you will all be despatched to wherever the need is.' He paused. 'See what a war does for you,' he said, attempting a feeble joke. 'You are being given the opportunity to do some travelling and see different places.'

As they moved away to resume their duties, Heather slipped her arm into Angelina's – Jane had gone back to the hut for something – and said, 'Wherever they do send us, Angelina, I really hope that we'll be together – you and me and Jane.' She paused. 'I know it's an awful thing to say, but I don't think I have ever been as happy in my life as I am now, even under these dreadful circumstances. We get on so well together, the three of us – and I feel I can do anything asked of me because you two are there, doing the same. I wouldn't have been capable of facing up to the horror of this war, the things we've been seeing, if I hadn't been able to glance up and see you and Jane there too.'

Angelina squeezed her arm. 'I know exactly what you mean, Heather,' she said, 'because we sort of give each other strength, don't we – helped quite a lot by Jane's sense of humour. We couldn't get through life if there wasn't something we could find to laugh about together.'

Heather smiled up gratefully. 'I'm glad you feel like that too, Angelina. Because, you see, I was never very good at making friends – at school, I mean. Everyone used to say that I was standoffish, but I was never that. It was that I just couldn't find the right things to say or do so that they would let me join in with them. I was always afraid of pushing myself in where maybe I wasn't really wanted,' Heather added. 'I was never invited to anyone's birthday parties, or things like that.'

Angelina shot her a look. 'Did you invite them to any of yours?'

'Oh, I never had a birthday party – not the sort you invite people to,' Heather said. 'Of course, I always had lovely presents, and then my parents and I would go out to afternoon tea some-where, or maybe to the theatre… as my treat. It was usually just the three of us because that's how we liked it.' She frowned briefly. 'I never thought to ask a friend to come along with us, because I was afraid they might not like to, and wouldn't know how to refuse.' She sighed. 'I never felt that anyone wanted to be my friend.'

'Well, there's never been any fear of that where *we* are concerned, Heather,' Angelina said firmly. 'We've been a trio since we first set our eyes on each other, haven't we, and nothing will ever change that. You mark my words! And when we get back home we'll spend hours and hours going over and over what we saw and did over here – we'll be in danger of boring everyone else to death!'

Christmas 1916

Despite the horror and death all around, it had been decided that Christmas should be celebrated as usual. Angelina glanced up at the others as they were all putting on their uniforms for the day.

'I know that St Thomas's was always decorated for the festive season,' she said, 'but it does feel strange seeing tinsel and baubles on the wards here – in these particular circumstances, I mean.'

The others agreed, but Heather said, 'Haven't you heard the patients singing carols? They seem quite prepared to enter into the spirit of the occasion, despite everything.'

'There are nearly as many Germans here now as English, and they have been singing "Holy Night" for days!' one of the others exclaimed, 'Some of them have got really nice voices.'

'Yes, I noticed that,' Jane said, 'and they seem very grateful for everything, don't they? Saying thank you over and over again and minding their manners. One of them has even said he would like to take me to his homeland after this is all over, and show me the sights! He told me that Berlin is a beautiful city.' She grinned. 'I told him I'd think about it.'

Angelina sighed briefly, thinking how quickly they'd got used to the German prisoners becoming part of them, part of the family. These soldiers were not foes anymore, they were human beings in need of care and attention, and their reaction to pain, or to how they were being treated, was exactly the same as any of the British Tommies. There was no difference.

By now, fewer casualties were coming in each week, and the blessed relief of comparative silence, without the incessant boom of the guns, had felt like an early Christmas present.

On Christmas Day, after Angelina and the others had done their rounds, everyone made their way to the canteen for dinner. The place had been transformed. Every corner had been decorated, there were even some balloons hanging from the roof struts of the huge tent, and there was popular music playing.

Jane nudged Angelina as they took their places at one of the tables. 'We have come from hell to heaven,' Jane said. 'Thank goodness there haven't been any really bad cases for a few days so we can eat our dinner in peace.'

And what a meal it was. Six courses, starting with soup, then fish and turkey with stuffing and all the trimmings, with Christmas pudding and brandy butter afterwards. It seemed almost too good to be true, but everyone tucked in, and presently the tables were moved to one side and the dancing began.

'I'll lead,' Jane said, automatically taking the role of male partner as she drew Angelina to her feet. It was a quick-step, and although Angelina hadn't had much experience of ballroom dancing, she picked it up pretty quickly, especially with Jane's robust direction.

They were dancing, war or no war, as if they didn't have a care in the world, and to Angelina there was a touch of incongruousness about it. But that was how it was, and for those few brief hours, time stood still. It was Christmas, they were going to enjoy it.

Presently, they were asked to leave as the tables had to be re-set for the staff who'd remained on duty to have their own meal. Much later, when Angelina and the others went back to the hut, their joy became even greater. Mail had arrived! The first they'd received since being in France. This had to be Santa Claus at his most benevolent!

The envelopes were there on the little table, and every nurse rushed forward to pounce on the one addressed to them.

There were two for Angelina, and she picked up hers, smiling at the address on the front of both, which read: 'Miss Angelina Green, a St Thomas's Hospital nurse, serving somewhere in France.' That was all they said, but they had arrived, and stretching out on her bed, Angelina began to read. The first one was from Miss Kingston, dated 10th August.

My dear Angelina

I am hoping this will reach you because of course we don't know where you are, but I have great faith in our Royal Mail and I'm sure they will come up trumps sooner or later.

Life here at the Garfield is much as usual, although some foodstuffs are becoming scarce. Mrs Haines had to queue for potatoes last week which I think came as rather a shock to her! But we are managing very well and all the children are as happy – and naughty! – as they usually are, bless them. You were never naughty, of course!

Mrs Marshall has not been very well lately, but she always turns up, come what may. I tell her to have some time off but she says she'd rather be at work.

I do think of you a lot, my dear. No one seems to know when this war will end, but my constant prayer is for your safety and wellbeing, and for that of your colleagues, too, of course. You are all very brave girls.

I know that Ruby is writing to you – she came here wanting to know where she should address the envelope. I do hope we've got it right. She is looking very bonny, so have no worries about her.

Take great care of yourself my dear girl. I think of you every day.

Sincerely, Miss Kingston

Angelina slid the letter back into the envelope, her eyes moist. It was the first time she'd been aware of homesickness, but it was aching inside her now. The Garfield, the only home she had ever known. She could almost smell it – Mrs Marshall's floor polish, Wright's coal tar soap in the basins, the smell of fresh laundry upstairs, the glorious scent of warm cakes cooling in the kitchen…

Angelina pulled herself together. Enough of that. There was still a lot of work ahead.

She opened the other envelope, noting how beautifully Ruby had written the address. Angelina wasn't surprised at that because Ruby had loved being taught to read and write, and the two of them had spent many happy hours together, poring over their books.

Dear Angelina

I wish I was talking to you, instead of writing! It seems ages since we were together.

I can't imagine all the stuff you are doing over there. I hear the war news from Mr and Mrs Walker and it sounds dreadful to me. Hairdressing is such a silly thing by comparison, but Mrs Walker says that we are keeping the home fires burning and that not everyone can go and fight.

I am so busy all the time that the days fly by. I am doing everything now, at the salon, and one or two customers ask for me specially. I thought Mrs Walker might be put out by this, but she isn't a bit. One morning we only had four clients so I was left completely in charge. I did feel very important! And didn't get anything wrong. I was given very generous tips!

The Carters are so sweet to me, Angelina. They're always asking me up for a cup of tea, or sometimes Sunday dinner, and of course I take over the baby. Nesta is absolutely gorgeous now, walking all over the place. She calls me 'Ooby'. I wonder how she will say your name when you come home!

As you can see, I am managing without my very best and dearest friend Angelina Green. Miss Jones has called in several times – just for a few minutes – and always brings cakes or biscuits to put in the tin. She says they'll keep me going!

So that's all my news, really.

I can't wait to see you again, Angelina. You will have such a lot to tell us.

Night night and God bless. And please, please, please, take care of yourself

Oodles and oodles of love,
Ruby.

P.S. I always leave Teddy in your bed. I know you left him for me, but he's yours, really, and I know he wants to be with you. So the nearest I can get is to tuck him under your pillow, but I always give him a kiss from you before we go to sleep. Xxxxx

Chapter 14

March 1917

Another cold and dreary month was passing, and the camp hospital became less frenetic as patients were fewer. Angelina and the others were thankful to be given the chance for a little more time off.

But it wasn't to last. At the beginning of April they were given their marching orders.

'You are all to go further up the Line,' Dr Lewis said as he consulted his file. 'Some to other field hospitals, and others to one of the Casualty Clearing Stations.' He glanced up. 'The stations are the noisier option because they are always close to the battle,' he said, 'but someone has to do it, and you are all pretty used to the sound of heavy warfare by now.'

Angelina wished he'd get on with it. 'So – who's going where?' she said. 'Are the same groups staying together?'

'Not necessarily,' the doctor said, 'but it looks as if you three—' he pointed to Angelina, Heather and Jane '—are to go to the stations, the others to one of the hospitals.' He paused briefly, not wishing to say that he had been asked which of the nurses he thought had the stomach for Casualty Clearing which was always a tough call. It seemed to him that Nurse Green and her two particular friends had become quite close and worked well together in the more extreme cases. A small band of nurses with a sense of humour thrown in. Perfect for Casualty Clearing.

They were going to be taken by truck or train at the end of the week. On Thursday evening, as they were enjoying a pot of tea in the canteen, Heather said, 'I'm really glad we are going to stay together, aren't you? We've become as close as sisters since we were all thrown into this mess.'

Jane nodded. "I wouldn't have believed how that might happen,' she said, 'because I've never been close to any other human being before in my life.' She grinned. 'So thanks to this bloody war, I've been given a novel experience!'

Angelina glanced at her quickly. It had been rather embarrassing to notice that Jane had been the only one in the hut who hadn't received any mail.

'No brothers or sisters for you, then, Jane?' Angelina enquired lightly.

'Oh no, and hardly any parents, either.' Jane looked away for a second. 'I don't want to sound pathetic because I couldn't give a damn anymore about the question of relationships, but as soon as I was born I was cast out into the wilderness of nannies and child minders… and private boarding school at the age of 7.' She cleared her throat. 'I mean, why would anyone bring a child into the world and then choose to ignore it? Pretend it isn't there? I will never forgive my mother and father for giving me everything that money can buy, and nothing else. No hugs and kisses and bedtime stories for me.' She curled her hands around her mug of tea before going on. 'Do you know the one thing that I will take with me to the grave? The day I was awarded a prize at the annual thanksgiving service at school. It was for "exceptional achievement in all subjects" – what do you think of that! I was so excited, and the assembly hall was packed with parents and grandparents and hangers on. But when I got up on to the stage and looked around for my parents, they were not there. They'd promised they would be coming but hadn't bothered to turn up and said afterwards that Daddy had an important meeting and that Mummy thought she had a cold coming.' Jane paused. 'I will never forget that feeling of utter desertion,' she said slowly. 'I was 10 years old, and no one had turned up to cheer for me.'

For a second, Angelina thought that Jane was going to shed a tear, but the moment passed and she grinned her usual hearty grin.

'So there's the story of my pathetic life,' she said, and Heather leaned forward and touched her hand.

'There is nothing at all pathetic about you or your life, Jane,' Heather said quietly. 'You may have felt deserted before, but we'll never desert you, will we, Angelina? We three will stay friends together until this is all over *and* after that – I *know* we will.' She smiled. 'I don't have any brothers or sisters either, but I do have very loving parents, and I would share them with you any day, Jane. You would love them, and they would love you because you're funny and you make us all laugh.'

Perhaps it was because of the uncertainty of what lay ahead that the feeling around the table was becoming maudlin, so Angelina said, 'Come on, sisters! We have to be up early in the morning so we'd better go and pack our few belongings.'

As they walked back to the hut, Heather, realising that Angelina had been rather quiet, said, 'Do you have sisters or brothers, Angelina?'

There wasn't a moment's hesitation. 'My background is like the rhyme, "There was an old woman who lived in a shoe, she had so many children she didn't know what to do, so she gave them some jam without any bread, smacked them all soundly and sent them to bed!"'

The others looked at her, astounded. 'Crumbs,' Jane said, 'are there that many of you at home? How marvellous. You must have had such fun growing up.'

Angelina nodded. 'I certainly did have a lot of fun,' she said. Then she decided it was time to come clean. 'No, it's not quite like that, it's just that I am an orphan – I was brought up in a large orphanage in the East End. I must have had parents, but I never knew who they were because apparently I just turned up and that was that.' She glanced at Jane. 'Perhaps my parents took one look at me and decided family life wasn't for them!'

Jane snorted. 'That's hardly likely. You must have been a very beautiful baby, Angelina.'

'Were they always kind to you... at the orphanage?' Heather said.

'Of course,' Angelina said, 'but we had our ups and downs. We used to fall out with each other and have scraps, but no one was allowed to be nasty.' She smiled. 'The nuns used to get cross and give us the cane sometimes and one of the helpers – Mrs Marshall – never liked me at all. When I tried to ask her things she'd tell me to buzz off and stop being a nuisance. But she was all right, really. And the priest, Father Laurence, he was another one! We had to sit very quietly and say prayers and learn the bible and then he'd test us to see if we'd been concentrating!'

'He sounds horrible,' Heather said, and Angelina shook her head.

'No, he wasn't horrible, and he gave me and my friend Ruby a blessing before we left, which was quite touching.' Angelina paused. 'He is very tall and sort of handsome, but he always looked rather sad to me.' She giggled. 'Our cook, Mrs Haines, can't bear him! I don't know why, but she and Mrs Marshall were always whispering about him.'

'When did you leave the orphanage?' Jane asked curiously. 'Was it when you started at St Thomas's?'

'No, before that,' Angelina replied. 'Orphans are only allowed to stay until they're fourteen, but they found a lovely little room in a nice house for me and my friend Ruby – we left at the same time – and they made sure we had jobs.'

'I can't imagine being brought up with dozens of others,' Heather said. 'There was always just me and my mother and father – and the cats. We've got four at the moment, and I've always had animals to play with, so I've never felt lonely, not really. But I've often thought that it would have been lovely to share a bedroom with someone and go on talking until we fell asleep. Still, the cats all curl up on my bed – and sometimes it can feel a bit crowded!'

'Do cats answer to their names?' Jane asked curiously. 'I mean, like dogs do?'

Heather smiled. 'Cats do exactly what they want, when they want,' she said. 'Sometimes they deign to look up when I speak to them, but mostly they live in their own little worlds, and I love them to death. They are my soul mates,' she added.

'So go on, tell us what these creatures are called,' Angelina said.

'They are Monty, Minty, Pepper and Beau, and although I don't have favourites – not really – Monty is a bit special because he was the first one I was given. I'm sure he feels he's the superior member of the gang!'

There were a few moments' silence as the three relaxed in the comparative comfort of the canteen, then Heather said, rather shyly, 'Do you mind if I ask you something, Angelina?'

'Ask away,' Angelina replied.

'It's just… it's just that… do you ever wonder about your parents? I mean, I've never been without mine – but do you ever wonder why yours were not able to care for you, or even what they might have looked like?' Heather looked away for a second. 'Sometimes you must have felt all alone in the world.'

Angelina didn't hesitate. 'No, I didn't feel alone in the world, Heather – because I was never by myself, you see. There were always others right there beside me, just the same as me – and I realise how lucky I was to have been taken in by the Garfield, the only home I have known. It was always very busy – and quite noisy!' Angelina smiled. 'But as a matter of fact, I do remember sometimes feeling that it *would* be nice to be by myself without constant company, especially at night, because I have never had a bedroom of my own. There was never enough room for that. And no, I don't remember wondering about my parents, not really. If I ever did think about who they might have been, my only thought was that they must have been very sad not to have brought me up themselves. Imagine having a baby, and then not watch it grow up,' she added.

'I... I hope you didn't mind me asking you that, Angelina,' Heather said quietly, 'but I've never met anyone like you before. You may be an orphan, but you're so positive, and... and happy all the time. Even over here! Whoever brought you into the world must have made sure that you came with all the qualities needed to survive – and thrive,' she added.

Jane half-stood, gathering up their empty mugs. 'While I would be the first to agree with that, Heather, I think we've proved that we've all been given enough backbone to see us through what we've had to face – and what's still ahead of us. So we must all thank our parents for that – even *me*! I suppose that when all is said and done, it's all in the genes!'

They made their way back to the hut, but much later, when they were all in bed and the others asleep, Angelina remembered only too well that there had been times when she'd pictured who her parents might have been and what they might have looked like.

Of course, she had no answers to those questions, but one thing Angelina was absolutely certain about. When she died and went to heaven, she would recognise her mother and father straightaway, and she would have so much to tell them! She would run towards them, and then they would collapse into each other's arms, laughing, and perhaps crying a bit with happiness, all talking at once...

And it would be as if they had never been parted. With that blissful thought in her heart, Angelina fell into a deep and dreamless sleep.

As soon as they arrived at the Casualty Clearing Station, the nurses had the responsibility of deciding which of the casualties should be sent straight on to field hospitals for treatment, or which of them should remain in the isolation unit until their infections were under control, And sadly, inevitably, there were those who were already beyond human help, and should be taken to the mortuary.

Almost at once, Angelina and Jane were instructed to stay and receive the ever-lengthening line of new wounded, while Heather was sent to the isolation unit. But at least, as before, the three were to share the same hut, so they had a little time to talk and share their day's experience.

Six days into this tour of duty began to feel more like six months to all the nurses as they dealt with the relentless tide of casualties making its way to comparative safety. The soldiers arrived straight from the trenches, and sometimes it was difficult to make out the features of the wounded as they were plastered in so much mud and blood.

For them, the station was the first sanctuary of any help and hope, and despite the tremendous noise from the battle raging just a few miles away, all those staggering on foot, or being helped by a comrade or being carried on stretchers, made their way forward with cheerful enthusiasm, as if, at last, they had escaped hell and had everything to look forward to.

But the medical staff was under no such illusion, because it was obvious that these were not just the wounded, they were often the dying, and no amount of care and attention was going to save them. And it was with a sick heart that, one day, when they were on duty together, Angelina said quietly to Jane, 'How can we help this poor boy, Jane? Where on earth do we start?'

The young soldier's face had been completely shot away, but he was still managing to move his arms and legs as if begging someone to notice him and give him a chance of life.

Jane pursed her lips at the question. 'We just do what we can and do our best,' she said. 'The last two casualties we checked out are obviously for the isolation unit. Heather said they were seeing more and more cases with badly infected wounds, brought straight from the stinking, earthy tombs the poor devils have been stuck in for weeks and weeks.'

'Yes, and apparently there are only two nurses on duty at any one time, so it's a busy

ward,' Angelina said. 'I thought poor Heather looked really stressed yesterday, which is unlike her.'

*

One Friday evening, after there'd been a lull in newcomers, Angelina, Heather and Jane managed to have an hour together in the canteen.

'Isn't it strange,' Angelina said, as they queued at the counter for tea and sandwiches, 'that despite all we've done and seen today – and all these terrible weeks – we can still manage to actually eat something?' She shrugged. 'It's true that I don't actually feel hungry, but I'm ready for a cheese sandwich.'

'Oh, I've never given up food,' Jane said, 'under any circumstances. And if we were silly enough to stop eating we'd be useless. You've got to take on fuel to keep going, whatever you're doing.'

They took their supper back to the table and sat down. By this time, the canteen was quite full, and despite the horror of their circumstances, everyone seemed able to chat, and there was some brief laughter now and again. After a while, noticing that Heather had only nibbled at the edge of her sandwich, Angelina she nudged her arm.

'What's the matter – not to your taste, Heather?'

Heather smiled quickly. 'I'm not hungry. But the tea is good,' she said, draining her mug, and Angelina stood up, taking it from her.

119

'I'll get you a refill.'

At the counter, Angelina glanced across, a worried expression on her face. To her, Heather looked unwell, not like herself at all, and for the last couple of days she'd developed a dry, persistent cough. But she'd waved away any comments.

'It's nothing,' she'd said, 'I've always been prone to this sort of thing.'

*

Three days later, Angelina and Jane sat by Heather's bed side at the staff hospital, gently wiping her forehead and trying to make her comfortable as her breathing became more and more laboured.

Neither of them spoke. There was nothing more to say to their friend whose life was slipping away before their eyes.

Nurse Heather Matthews had been nursing soldiers affected by blue pus – the vile infection brought back from the trenches – and now, she had developed double pneumonia.

Presently, the doctor on duty came over to the bed, and after a few moments he glanced at the two friends sitting either side. He shook his head.

'I'm sorry,' he said quietly. Suddenly, for the first time for many hours, Heather tried to sit up, grasping Angelina's hand.

'I can't find Monty,' Heather whispered faintly. 'I don't know where he is!' She began to cry. 'Please help me find him, Angelina, please! He should be here, on my bed... please...'

Both girls leaned forward to console her, and Jane said, in her usual clear way, 'Don't you worry, Heather! We know exactly where Monty is and we're going to fetch him back to you now, straightaway. Okay? Angelina and Jane, your two sisters, are on the case! Just leave it to us!'

Heather collapsed back on to her pillow and smiled faintly. 'Thank you,' she whispered. 'Oh look! Here he is! Monty! Bad boy! You know I don't like you straying… that's right, you curl up by me and keep warm…'

An hour later, with Angelina and Jane holding her hands, Heather died peacefully in her sleep.

Chapter 15

Why had it never occurred to her that any one of them might
become ill and die, Angelina asked herself over and over again?
Doctors and nurses were supposed to be invincible, weren't they?
They were here with all the answers to treat the sick and wounded,
not to fall by the wayside.

But watching gentle Heather slip away from them like that
had been the harshest lesson yet for Angelina. By now, she had
seen many pass away, but not someone she had grown to love
and care about. Losing Heather had been unthinkable, and
for days afterwards it had been difficult to continue the job
without wanting to run away and hide somewhere, anywhere.
To escape.

But there was no escape; the terrible routine continued as if
nothing had happened, as if she, Heather and Jane were still there
in the hut together in the evenings, talking, sharing their thoughts
and hopes and fears Instead, Heather had been taken miles away
from them, to rest in an English cemetery on French soil.

Then, months later, one miserable, wet day in August, something happened that Angelina could only have imagined in her
wildest dreams.

Their group of nurses had come to the end of receiving the

latest contingent of the wounded, and Angelina suddenly stopped short. What was that? What had she just heard?

It was the sound of a voice calling her name, a voice so familiar, yet so far from her thoughts that for a second she thought she was hallucinating. But there it was again.

'Angelina.'

The warm, deep tone was unmistakable, and she turned quickly to find what – who – she was looking for.

'Angelina?'

And there he was, standing a short distance away. Tall, handsome, Alexander Garfield in an officer's uniform, his eyes alight with recognition.

For the briefest moment time stood quite still, then as if her feet had wings, Angelina almost threw herself forward towards him, and he put out his arm to stop her from tumbling and held her to him in a brief hug. He looked down at her and their eyes met.

'I cannot believe what I am seeing,' he said, his voice husky. 'It is you, Angelina, my dear girl, isn't it? You aren't a mirage?'

She smiled a wobbly smile, hoping that she wasn't going to burst into tears. Which of God's angels had decided that she and Alexander Garfield were to meet in this place and under these circumstances?

'Oh, Mr Alexander,' she said. 'I had no idea, I mean, I didn't know you had even enlisted…'

He smiled a trifle wearily, still holding her close. 'There was no option, really. It was obviously my duty.' He paused. 'Besides, I'd been told you were in uniform, Angelina. What would you have thought of me if I'd stayed nice and safe at home while you were over here doing your bit?'

She was still looking up at him but moved away slightly, suddenly embarrassed that they were standing so close. He was still Mr Garfield's son, and she just one of the orphans who'd been rescued. But their mutual reaction had been instinctive and natural. Two old friends finding momentary comfort in each other

123

under terrible conditions. She realised that for those brief seconds she had been nearer, physically, to Alexander Garfield than ever before in her life, and it had taken this war, this stinking war, to make a dream come true. She cleared her throat.

'Are you going to be here for long, Mr Alexander?' she said, and he shook his head.

'No – I'm back on the front line straightaway,' he said. 'The reason I'm here is that I was the only officer available to lead the small group accompanying our wounded to the Clearing Station. It's a job I like to avoid if I can,' he added, 'but if I'd known I'd be coming across you – I mean, meeting someone from home – I might have been more enthusiastic!'

His dark eyes looked her up and down, and he half-smiled. 'I must say that outfit suits you very well, Angelina,' he said. 'You look very neat and competent and... *very* important! Absolutely perfect for the job in hand!'

She glanced down, flicking a hand over her skirt. 'As a matter of fact, I happen to be wearing the uniform which has just been cleaned, and which I only picked up from the laundry yesterday, so it is still comparatively decent. But – I'm glad you approve,' she added shyly.

Suddenly, Jane's voice from a short distance away interrupted them. 'Angelina, I've just been told that there's another batch arriving in about an hour, so time for a quick bite first. Are you coming?'

'Coming!' Angelina called back. She glanced up at Alexander. 'Sorry, I have to go. That's how it is here I'm afraid, hardly any time to catch your breath, or even to know what day it is...'

She knew she was stumbling over her words but she couldn't help it. She was standing in the middle of a foreign field with Alexander right there beside her, and neither of them knew if they were ever to meet again, or what might happen to either of them. Even as those thoughts formed in her head she felt her knees tremble slightly. She turned to go, then glanced back.

'I feel so... so... happy that we met each other, Mr Alexander,' she said. 'Who would have thought that we'd end up in the same patch of nightmare – even for a few moments – and actually come face to face?'

He moved forward quickly then and grasped her hand. 'Wait... wait a minute,' he said. 'Look, I don't intend taking the team back until much later... perhaps about eleven o'clock, so is it possible that somehow, somewhere, we could have a longer chat, Angelina?' He shook his head briefly. 'The odds against us actually meeting were massive – unthinkable – so we mustn't lose this chance to talk, to... you know, catch up, talk about home. Please say that you can get away for just a couple of hours – tonight – this evening? They must surely give you some time off?'

His pleading took her by surprise, and for the first time she noticed how less than perfect he looked, saw the streaks of mud on his uniform, saw his hair, his beautiful dark hair wet and slightly matted in the front. How vulnerable he suddenly appeared. She smiled up at him.

'Each new batch of wounded usually takes us a few hours to clear,' she said, 'but it's only midday now, so with a bit of luck I should be free later on. I can't really promise, but it's possible that we could meet in the canteen – perhaps about nine o'clock?' She made a face. 'If I don't arrive I can only apologise, but I'll do my best, Mr Alexander, I really will.'

His grasp of her hand tightened. 'I understand, of course I do,' he said. 'But I will be there, I promise you, and I'll hang on until the last minute in case you turn up.' He gazed down at her. 'Why do you keep calling me Mr Alexander?' he said. 'I am Alexander, Angelina, and we are old friends. We know each other too well for any formalities, please... I am Alexander. So remember that. Okay?'

She smiled briefly. 'All right,' she said, hoping that she would remember the headmasterly instruction. He had been Mr

Alexander all her life – all their lives. Could they really bridge the gap that had separated them for so long?

*

It was gone eight o'clock before Angelina and Jane made their way back to their hut. It had been a grueling afternoon, with more casualties than usual arriving, stretcher after stretcher, with the walking wounded stumbling alongside in an endless stream. All the wards were full, the mortuary nearly so.

'I'm thankful that's over,' Jane announced as she opened the door of the hut. 'I was just about ready to hand in my resignation!'

'Oh Jane, don't say things like that,' Angelina said, following her inside. 'I don't think I could go on without knowing that you're here too.' She glanced across. 'I don't think I will ever get over losing Heather so quickly. It's still hard to believe that she's no longer here as well.'

Jane flopped down on her bed and stretched out. 'Don't let's get maudlin, old thing,' she said. 'That's all we need. But what I want to know is how you managed to get that male hunk talking to you this morning! I saw you! What a smasher! You were obviously finding lots to say to each other and I was so jealous I nearly came across and scratched your eyes out.'

Angelina couldn't help smiling. Jane never missed a thing.

'You will find this hard to believe, Jane,' Angelina said as she bent over to take off her shoes, 'but the hunk you mention is someone I've known all my life.'

Jane interrupted. 'Really? How incredible that you should meet up in this God-forsaken hell hole.' She whistled through her teeth. 'I only wish I had an old friend like that – tall, dark and handsome hardly covers it, does it?'

Angelina didn't reply to that, but said casually, 'His name is Alexander Garfield, and his father, Mr Randolph, owns the orphanage where I was brought up. I've known Alexander since

126

we were both little. He's a few years older than me and he used to visit the orphanage quite a lot – especially in the early days. I haven't seen him so much lately,' she added, 'because I left the orphanage when I was 14 – as I mentioned the other day – and he's been away at college for several years.'

Jane yawned loudly. 'Well, from the way he was looking at you this morning, I think he has missed you rather a lot!' She turned to glance at Angelina. 'You seemed rather overwhelmed, too, if I may say so. It's a shame that they're not going to be here for long, or you might have got off with him!'

Angelina turned and smiled. 'Well, I did think there might be just an hour or two to see him again,' she said lightly, 'so I promised to meet him in the canteen about nine, if I possibly could. I said it might be difficult, though.'

'Well, in that case, you'd better go straight to the wash house and get cleaned up,' Jane said decisively. 'What are you going to wear to impress this Adonis!'

*

Just before nine o'clock, Angelina made her way the few hundred yards to the canteen. It was a warm evening and it hadn't rained for several hours, so the well-trodden grass was soft under her feet.

The nurses had brought very few of their own clothes with them, and from the few things she did have, Angelina had chosen her deep blue cotton skirt – the length just below the knee – and her white, frilly blouse with the small, rounded sleeves that caressed her slim shoulders. She was wearing her white pumps, and was carrying only her small clutch purse to hold a hanky and a little money. While showering, she had made sure that her hair was shampooed and thoroughly rinsed so that there was no trace of dirt or dust lingering amongst her long tresses. However much you tried, it was hard to remain absolutely clean for long. She had left her hair loose – a change from the normally severely clipped-back style demanded of all the nurses.

As she approached the canteen, she saw that the door was wide open. Light chattering and laughter could be heard, and all of a sudden Angelina felt her heart lurch with apprehension. She felt as if she was going on a first date! But how would that feel, anyway? She had never had a first date, or any date, with a man. And anyway, it wasn't as if she was meeting a stranger – she was going to be spending a brief hour or so with a member of her family... well, sort of her family. So why was her heart racing as if she was about to sit another exam?

But she wished he hadn't instructed her to leave out the Mr Alexander. Somehow, being more familiar with him was going to leave her feeling as if she was taking liberties.

As she entered, she didn't have to look around for him because there he was, standing up by a table in the far corner, his hand raised to catch her attention. As soon as she approached, he pulled out a chair for her, and they both sat down opposite each other.

'Thank heaven you were able to make it,' he said, looking across at her. Then, after a pause: 'I've been biting my fingernails that it wasn't going to happen and that this morning would be the last I'd see of you until the war was over.'

He was still in his uniform, but Angelina saw that it had been brushed clean, and he, too, had obviously washed his hair because it looked and smelt wonderful. She lowered her eyes briefly, hoping he hadn't noticed her flushed cheeks. He broke the spell by referring to what they might have to eat.

'What would you like, Angelina? What can I get you?' He raised one dark eyebrow. 'This is not the Ritz or the Savoy hotel – as you obviously already know – but I went over to the counter when I came in and I thought the sliced ham looked good, and the salad seems fresh. I was told that the bread rolls have just come over from the bakery. Shall we have any of that? You must be hungry, and I could eat something. But how about a drink first? I shall have a beer, but would you like a glass of wine?'

Angelina didn't hesitate, even though she'd never drunk alcohol before, thinking that she wasn't likely to be affected after just one glass, and anyway – who cared if she was! Alexander would see her safely back to the hut.

'A glass of white wine is exactly what I need,' she said coolly.

Alexander went over to the counter to order what they wanted, then came back carrying the two drinks.

''They're bringing the food in a minute,' he said, and Angelina raised her eyes.

'Really?' she said. 'We don't usually get waiter service here! How did you manage that?' She took the glass of wine from him and was about to take a sip when he stopped her, touching her hand lightly.

'Of any event I have ever attended in my life, Angelina,' he said seriously, 'this is one that calls for a toast.' He raised his glass and clinked it against hers. 'To us, and our unbelievable good luck in seeing each other here. And, please God, to our continuing safety until we're home again.'

'To us, and to our safety until we are home,' Angelina repeated. Then they both drank, and as Angelina felt the bubbles teasing her tongue, the cooling sensation of the wine as it slipped down her throat, she wished that she could stop the clock, now! She wanted to stay here for ever with Alexander, just the two of them. War or no war, for a few moments she was drifting on a cloud of pure happiness. She didn't want it to end, because she was living a dream! One of the many dreams like this that she had had in her life.

Presently their food arrived, and after they had eaten, Alexander sat back and looked across. 'Which of us is going to start?' he said easily.

For the next few minutes they exchanged news of when and how they'd arrived in France, and some of what they'd experienced, though neither giving too many details of what they'd so far seen and endured. Then memories of all the Christmases at The Garfield came up, and how Miss Kingston always kept the place running like a well-oiled machine.

The canteen was quieter now, many people having drifted away, and Alexander – who hadn't taken his eyes off Angelina for some time – said, 'Have you received any news from home? It's all very scanty, of course, but I did hear from my father in answer to a letter he received from me.'

'I've only had two,' Angelina said. 'One from Miss Kingston and one from my friend, little Ruby. Do you remember Ruby, Mr Alexander?'

He leaned forward and smiled, tapping her hand. 'Have you forgotten what I want you to call me?'

She smiled back. 'Sorry – but it's very hard not to use the name I have always known you by. So I will ask you again – do you remember Ruby... Alexander?'

He nodded. 'That's more like it. And of course I remember Ruby. She was a very introverted little thing, wasn't she? Seemed to cling to you like a Siamese twin. Miss Kingston always kept my father up to date with news of his... of his children,' Alexander went on, 'and I've sometimes thought that his orphans filled the gap caused by the fact that my mother died young, denying my parents the pleasure of having any more of the offspring they'd apparently wanted.' Alexander grinned suddenly. 'My father's had to put up with just me around all these years, poor chap.'

Angelina gazed up at him as he spoke, admiring for the umpteenth time in her life his fine features, the strength of his brow, his uncompromising mouth, and those dark, dark eyes which had always seemed to enter her very soul.

He glanced at his watch and stood up suddenly. 'It's almost time for me to check on my team because we'll soon be on the move,' he said reluctantly. 'But...' he looked down at Angelina.

'Could we possibly have a short stroll somewhere first? Or are you too tired?'

Angelina stood as well. 'I'm not too tired,' she said. 'In fact, Jane – my colleague – and I often take a short walk away from the place, to free ourselves for a few minutes and pretend that we're anywhere but here! And we always end up in the same field,' she added as they left the canteen. 'It's a short distance from here, and it has a little stream at the end which has a tree trunk across it acting as a bridge.' She smiled. 'We haven't actually sat on that yet because so far it's always been too wet and the stream is usually quite full, so we don't particularly want to fall in and get soaked.'

They were strolling very close together now, almost touching, soon reaching the long field Angelina had described. It had a five-barred gate, and Alexander pushed it open for them both to go in.

By now, it was almost dark, and whether she almost lost her footing, or whether her glass of wine was suddenly taking effect, Angelina stumbled and fell against Alexander and he immediately put his arm around her.

'Careful,' he murmured. 'Even though you must be as light as a feather, it would be a long way for me to carry you back.'

Leaning into him, Angelina looked up apologetically. 'Sorry,' she said, 'I'm used to wearing slightly tougher footwear than these pumps and—'

But before she could utter another word his lips had closed over hers and he was kissing her, gently at first, then a little more urgently, and Angelina felt her senses swimming. What was going on? What was happening? Surely another dream of hers wasn't coming true! But even as those thoughts entered her mind, she felt herself kissing him back. She'd never kissed anyone like this before, anyone at all! But it was easy. It was lovely… it was beautiful. And she didn't want it to stop!

Then Angelina came to her senses. This might be beautiful, but it was wrong! She had no right, no business, to be held by Alexander like this, to be close to him like this, to want him like

131

this! Because he was promised to someone else. Everyone knew that. He already had a woman in his life, and that life could never include her, Angelina Green! Why should it? How could it? So what were they doing, clinging to each other like this! It made no sense! She tried to pull away.

'Please… Alexander, please,' she whispered. 'I'm so sorry, I really am. But we should not be doing this, this should not be happening…'

But he wouldn't let her go, holding her even more tightly. 'Don't be sorry, because I'm not sorry, Angelina,' he murmured into her ear. 'I'm not sorry at all.'

Then his lips found hers again, and despite all her finer feelings, she melted into his arms, loving the feel of his rough tunic against her skin, of his face so close to hers. This was what she had wanted, for so long, but why had it taken a war to make it happen? And what had happened to her, Angelina Green, orphan, that what she felt ready for at this heady moment was the weight of him on her, the feel of his hands exploring her naked body. If he made that happen she knew she was ready to respond, to receive his maleness completely and without inhibition.

She gazed up at him, waiting for the illusion to pass, waiting to wake up and find that it had been a dream, after all. But the strength of his body close to hers was proof enough. They were here now, and she was in his arms, and although she knew it would never, could never, happen again, it would be enough. It would have to be enough.

Alexander Garfield had arrived by her side at just the right time to help Angelina accept the horror of her friend's sudden death. The cold stain of sorrow was being lifted, as if by magic, by the warmth of being loved, of being caressed, by the closeness of the here and the now, to the living, rather than being shackled by the dark pain of bereavement.

Chapter 16

March 1918, and the months that followed would always be known as the ultimate personification of hell. The war raged on with the Germans advancing all the time and the allies retreating. Roads and railways had been bombed out of existence, and it seemed to those sremaining at the forefront of battle that this could be the end of the world.

Sadly for them both, Angelina and Jane were separated and sent to different field hospitals, but they promised to always remain friends and keep in touch. If they were lucky enough to get out of this alive… Because by now, the realisation had fully dawned on Angelina that although, as nurses, they were not actually in military uniform, the fact remained that they were all within reach of sudden, violent death.

But if they did make it back home, the three girls had made a pact that they'd stay close, and in their hearts Heather, too, would always be there beside them. Time would never eradicate the memory of all they had done, all they had seen, all they had been through together.

By now, Angelina was carrying out her daily and nightly duties in a manner which was becoming almost robotic. There was nothing she hadn't seen before, but thankfully, these days she rarely came across severe head injuries, owing to the soldiers now all wearing tin helmets. That had not been the case when she'd first come to France, and head injuries had been the most prolific and the most horrific.

One night, lying on her bed after a long shift, Angelina asked herself a serious question. Was she now so able, so competent at the job, so aware of her own ability to deal with everything that faced her on an hourly basis, that she no longer felt herself wanting to shut her eyes at the sight and sounds of her injured, delirious patients? That she could do what she had to do without having to force herself to stay calm, as she had in the beginning? Had she come to the point that Heather's father had spoken of? To treat these soldiers as mere dummies? Had she actually become immune to the dreadful suffering she had encountered and was still witnessing day after endless day? Was that what nursing really was – not to feel anything at all? Had her quiet confidence turned her into an unfeeling nurse?

Angelina turned over, pulling her pillow more closely under her neck. No, she had not come to that point she told herself fiercely. All the soldiers she had ever treated could have been sick children of her own. Or like brothers, and friends, links in the unbreakable chain of common humanity.

1918 struggled along its inexorable path until towards its end it became obvious that there was only one way out. At last, Germany reluctantly agreed to sign a truce with Britain and France that there should be no more fighting on either side. The war had almost reached an end.

11th November 1918

The late autumn day was cold, the sort of cold that chilled every bone, a stiffening breeze causing the few remaining leaves on the trees to drift down to the wet and soggy undergrowth. There was no birdsong in that secluded corner of the forest, adding to the overpowering sense of melancholy.

Huddled inside the only shelter for many miles around were eight men, all in uniform. Four of them, unsmiling, faced each other across a wooden table, the others stood, watchfully, a few steps behind. The atmosphere was stiff with tension and there was little conversation.

Then the oldest man in the group, leaning on his cane, moved forward slightly and lowered his gaze, once more, to the row of papers placed neatly in front of him. He picked up the pen which lay there and slowly, with great deliberation, wrote his signature before moving aside for the other three to add their own.

Now some gentle murmuring took place, breaking the silence, before the entire group made its way outside, going carefully down the few steps to face a photographer waiting to capture the scene for posterity.

In the continuing gloom of that grey day there was no sign of triumph or elation. For one in the gathering, particularly, the suffocating mantle of his country's prospects was already bearing down with an unbearable heaviness. For the rest, only a regretful sadness filled their hearts and minds.

It was over, but what a dreadful price had been paid.

Somewhere on the Belgian front, and deep underground, the enveloping fetid stench of mould drifted like a damp, cloying curtain, filling the nostrils of the men waiting for the next instruction, the next command. Perhaps, this time, it would be the last one they would hear before they met their Maker.

Alexander Garfield, the young officer in charge, was half-standing, half-leaning against the mud wall. His men were lying down, legs outstretched, chins on their chests, trying to catch some sleep. The only one fully awake was sitting up, his bent knees providing a rest for the pad on which he was writing his poetry, the poetry which had stopped him from going mad over the weeks and months of combat.

Suddenly, one long, strident ring from the field telephone made the officer immediately straighten up and move the few steps to reach it. The others barely bothered to rouse themselves, but they were listening, wary…

The message was short, and the officer's reply equally so. 'Repeat?' And then, more quietly, 'Roger.'

Then, leaving the receiver dangling on its wire, he gazed down at the others. 'It's over,' he said flatly. 'The armistice was signed this morning.'

He might have expected whoops and cheers from his men but only a stunned silence greeted his words before they could bring themselves to believe the longed-for news.

Going over the top, his gun at the ready, Garfield stared around him, stared at the open expanse of desecrated countryside, stared into the grey silence, waiting. At last, the news which he himself had not dared to believe, struck home and he stood up, dropping his gun by his side – just as he saw a German soldier begin heaving himself up from a dug out in the ground.

Garfield raised his voice. 'It's over!' he shouted. 'Drop your weapon! The war is over!'

At first the German did not believe the news and instinctively raised his gun. Until he saw the British officer begin slowly walking forward, his arms outstretched in greeting, and heard the repeated news – 'The war is over, my friend! The truce was signed this morning! Praise God! We are all going home!'

Shaking with relief, the two embraced as brothers and both sobbing helplessly, fell to the ground in each other's arms.

*

Angelina lay down on her bed and stared up at the ceiling, her feelings a torment of mixed emotions. So, it was all over, then. But nobody had won. It had merely been agreed that it was fruitless to continue the fight.

She glanced across at the other beds, which were empty. Only four nurses shared this hut, rather than six, and the other three must have gone off somewhere to celebrate the news which they'd heard this morning. There had been rumours before that the war was about to end, but now it was fact.

The world was apparently at peace.

Angelina hadn't wanted to join the other nurses over at the canteen. If Jane – and Heather – were here, it would have been different, but, Angelina had not become particularly close to her new companions. For one thing, they seldom seemed to be on the same ward at the same time, and they didn't often meet when they were off duty, either.

None of this mattered to Angelina. If it couldn't be their old trio, she would rather spend her time alone. And now that all the blood had been shed and all those lives lost, she felt only a sense of pointlessness, rather than a sense of euphoria. It was like the Somme, all over again. Nothing had been gained, but so much lost.

If any of them had thought that they could start packing up to go home, they were soon to realise that, for quite some time, it would be business as usual. The huge backlog of wounded and dying soldiers would be passing through their hands for many months to come, but still, at least the incessant din of battle had stilled, replaced, overwhelmingly, by birdsong. Soon, it was possible to actually be aware of other, gentler, sounds, of the sounds of nature.

But during the first hours and weeks of peace, for Angelina, her overriding thoughts were for Alexander. She had heard nothing from him, or about him, for sixteen months, not since that magical evening when they'd been together. Had he been wounded – or had he even managed to survive? The thought that it was possible that they would never see each other again was too terrible to contemplate.

*

The entire country, and London in particular, went mad with rejoicing. All the schools closed, shops and factories were shut, and in the streets and even on the roofs of cars, Land Girls and servicemen and women danced together in gay abandon. Trains and busses hooted, flags fluttered from office windows and huge crowds made their way along Whitehall towards Downing Street, all singing, and chanting. It had been a long, long wait.

At the Garfield, the atmosphere was just as frantic. The older children had a very good idea as to why everyone was so excited, and why Mrs Haines kept wiping her eyes on her apron, and why lessons were abandoned and why they were playing games instead and why sweets and chocolates were being handed around as if it was someone's birthday.

At home in his study, Randolph Garfield gazed out with a heart full of gratitude. His beloved son had escaped the carnage with his life intact. Or so Randolph fervently hoped. They had not seen each other for almost two years, and news of any kind had always been scant. He had been told that demobilisation would take place as quickly as possible, but Randolph was happy enough to wait his turn.

Alexander was alive and that was all that mattered.

Chapter 17

April 1919

Angelina finished wiping up their breakfast dishes, then went over to the window and gazed out. Ruby had left for work long ago, and the little room felt deserted and lonely without her here. It had been obvious, straightaway, to Angelina just how her little friend had matured while they'd been apart. Ruby seemed so happy and content with her lot, and apparently Mrs Walker had said she was sure that Ruby would have a salon of her own one day.

Angelina smiled as she went over what had happened when she'd walked through the door, unannounced, ten days ago – there'd been no opportunity to give notice of her return. Ruby had stared as if she'd seen a ghost, then she'd burst into tears, hugging Angelina over and over again, and wailing loudly like a baby. Mrs Carter, with Nesta in her arms, had heard the noise and had come running down the stairs, and then they had all cried, Angelina included. Tears of uninhibited joy.

It was then that Angelina realised that those were the first tears she'd shed in so long. She'd never been a cry baby as a child, and she didn't even cry when Heather had slipped away – refusing to show any sign of outward emotion or lack of self-control. Because if you opened that box, how would you ever manage to close it?

Angelina sat down slowly onto her bed, and recalled – for the hundredth time – that moment when she had completely lost her self-control.

It had been when she and Alexander Garfield had fallen into each other's arms and kissed. His bodily strength as he'd held her close to him, his fervent lips on hers. It had been an oasis of pure ecstasy amongst the desert of hopelessness all around them on that weary battlefront.

But it had been wrong. She should never have let it happen. Because they could never be anything to each other. Their situations in life could not have been more different even though he had always treated her with such sweet kindness, as if he cared for her, cared about her.

But that was just his nature, and when they had been so close on that day, his response had been a purely natural, masculine thing. Angelina understood that only too well. It hadn't been full of meaning, as it had been for her. It had been a male, passing need which he probably, by now, didn't even remember. There was no doubt about where he would find his future solace. Honora Mason would be here, faithful and loving as always.

All the nurses had been given a month off to recover from their war duty before they were to return to St Thomas's at the beginning of May. Then, it was expected that life would return to some kind of normality.

And although Angelina admitted that she had been as excited as anyone else at the thought of returning home, now that she was here she could not deny a sense of anticlimax. For a long time she had been with a faithful band of people who'd become close as they'd worked together as a team to treat the wounded and dying – of course she was going to miss all that. It would take time to readjust. Hadn't dear Miss Kingston warned her of that possibility when Angelina had called in at the orphanage on her return?

'Take your time, Angelina,' the superintendent had said gently. 'You have been living a completely unimaginable life – something which none of us can hope to fully understand – so take each day at a time and try not to look back or forward too much.'

Angelina felt cross with herself as she wandered about the little room aimlessly, trying to find something to do. She should be making the most of this last couple of weeks, not keeping on going over and over all that had happened to her, to all of them. Especially as, during her one brief homecoming visit to the hospital, she'd been told that the influenza pandemic which had been raging for more than a year was still in full swing.

In the almoner's office, the matron and the senior staff had welcomed the nurses back, congratulating all of them on their distinguished service to the country.

'You have done St Thomas's proud,' matron had declared, 'but I'm afraid your responsibilities are still as great as ever. We are losing patients on a regular basis with this illness, so I am afraid that once you have had your time off it will be back to normal with a vengeance.'

July 1919

Alexander Garfield strolled home along the quiet streets he'd known all his life, his overwhelming feeling being gratitude that he was actually here alive and all in one piece. There had been many times when he'd felt death so near that he'd become resigned to the thought that foreign earth would be where his body would permanently rest.

Yet here he was, just a hundred yards away from the elegant house where he'd been brought up, and where he knew his father would be waiting for him.

Alexander's unit had been one of the last to be demobilised, and although word had been sent to Randolph of his son's imminent arrival, Alexander had asked that no one should meet him, that he would prefer to spend a few hours totally alone with his thoughts. Being in close company with others for so long, under such violent circumstances, had drained Alexander, and now all he wanted was isolation and peace.

Arriving, he made his way up the stone steps to the pillared entrance, but before he could ring the bell the door opened and Randolph stood there.

'Hello Dad,' Alexander said quietly.

Without speaking, Randolph clutched his son to him so closely that Alexander could hardly breathe. 'You are here, my dear boy,' Randolph said huskily. 'Praise God, you have returned to home and hearth... and to your father who has missed you more than words can say.'

Alexander didn't pull away, unsurprised at the words of welcome. Although he had spent much of his life away at school and college, and although Randolph was sometimes viewed as being of a serious nature, Alexander had suffered no dearth of affection when he'd been young.

Reluctantly, Randolph stood back and ushered Alexander inside. It was mid-afternoon on a warm day... how did you welcome someone back from the dead? Randolph cleared his throat. 'Where do we start, Alexander? Can you bear to talk, or shall we just sit here for a while? Or would you prefer a bath and a few hours upstairs on your own?'

It was a strange situation, Randolph thought. He had always been close to his only child, yet here, today, they could have been two people who hardly knew each other. Why wasn't conversation flowing, why weren't they falling over their words?

Alexander broke the silence. 'I don't want anything at the moment, Dad, thanks – I had a coffee at the station, but maybe we can indulge in something stronger later on.' He ran a hand through his hair 'Now you tell me how you've been. Has the firm survived, despite everything? The war hasn't bankrupted Garfield Tobacco, has it?'

Randolph shrugged briefly. 'No of course not, though we've had problems, naturally. But worse, this wretched pandemic has really taken everyone by surprise. It began a year ago, and it's still sweeping the country – and other parts of the world, I believe.'

Alexander nodded. 'Yes, we were all aware of it.'

There was a brief silence, then Randolph said, without looking at his son, 'I expect you called in to the Masons' on your way here – to see Honora?'

'No, I didn't,' Alexander replied. 'All I wanted was to see you, Dad. To come home.'

Randolph nodded, pleased at that. 'Oh well. Naturally they've been contacting me relentlessly once I told them you were on your way,' he said. 'I did expect that Honora would be the first one to actually set eyes on you.' He smiled. 'I expect she thought so, too! I believe that Elizabeth has made an iced cake to celebrate your return – they want to throw a party for you.'

'That's kind,' Alexander said, stifling a yawn.

Randolph had been watching his son's every move as they sat opposite each other in the quiet drawing room. Alexander seemed to look older than his 22 years – older, introspective, withdrawn. Of course, that was no surprise – how could anyone go through what those men had endured and come away unblemished? Even if Alexander had apparently escaped any serious injury, there would be underlying things he was dealing with. He had always been a little bit too sensitive, and he would have seen and done things which would remain in his memory until the end of his days. This war would have changed him, and many other people.

Presently, Randolph said, 'Have you had a chance to even give a thought as to what your next step is, Alexander? I mean, you don't have to return to college… you could stay home for as long as you like, take it easy, take your time making up your mind about your future.'

Alexander raised his eyes, surprised at the question. 'Oh, I intend continuing my studies, Dad – but I'd like to switch to something else.'

Randolph nodded. 'Of course. You don't need to continue your business studies course if you don't want to. But what else do you have in mind?'

'I'd like to go into medicine,' Alexander said promptly. 'I've thought about it such a lot while I've been away... the things I've seen.' He waited before going on. 'I know I could be of more use to humanity than doing what I have been doing, and you know I was always good at physics and maths. The thing is, it will be a very long training – probably six years or more – and I realise you might have liked me to go into the firm with you, but—'

Randolph sat forward, interrupting. 'No, Alexander. That was never my wish for you – unless you had really wanted it. All I've ever wanted is that you spend your life doing something you want to do, and become good at it.' Randolph smiled. 'And don't worry about the length of time that degree will take you – Garfield Tobacco will support you until you start earning your own cash.'

*

Two weeks later, after a superb dinner at the Masons' mansion, Jacob Mason stood at the head of the table and tapped his glass.

'Ladies and gentlemen,' he said ponderously, 'I think the time has come to drink a toast to our gallant serviceman on his safe return from combat.'

The gathering, consisting of Randolph and Alexander, Jacob, Elizabeth and Honora Mason, Jacob's accountant and his wife, and Honora's best friend Alice, all stood up obediently.

'To Alexander,' Jacob announced. 'Congratulations on your

service to our country, and our heartfelt thanks and relief that you have returned to us safe and sound.'

'Alexander!' everyone chanted.

Then they all drank and sat down again and resumed chatting, and Honora said quietly to Alexander who was sitting alongside her, 'Sorry about that, Alexander. You know what Dad's like.'

Alexander smiled down at her. 'He means well,' he murmured. 'It's good to see you again – and I like what you're wearing.'

Honora shrugged. 'My mother was determined that I should buy something new to welcome you home,' she said, 'but I thought I had enough clothes already, and anyway – I didn't think you'd notice what I was wearing. I imagine you have far weightier things to occupy your mind.' She glanced up. 'Do you know, you've hardly said a word about what you went through, Alexander. Was it dreadful… was it terrible?'

'That just about sums it up,' Alexander said. 'And perhaps I will talk about it one day.' He took a drink from his glass. 'I'd far rather talk about you and what you've been doing for the last two or more years, Honora.'

'Not winning a war, I'm ashamed to say,' Honora said. 'But, you know, well… just going around with my mother and helping with her various charities. I even had to chair a meeting for her the other day because she had a headache.' Honora paused. 'Can I let you into a secret, Alexander? Sometimes… sometimes, I really wished that I was in uniform and carrying a gun like you. Doing something important. Something that had some point to it.' She slid her glass across to touch Alexander's. 'I would like some of your courage… some of your strength.'

Alexander's eyes softened. He'd never heard Honora say things like this before.

'And are you going back to your studies in September?' Honora asked, 'Am I going to have to wave you goodbye again?'

''Fraid so,' Alexander said, deciding not to mention his change of direction. That would all come out in the wash.

145

At the other end of the long table, Jacob Mason nudged his wife.

'Just look at those two, Elizabeth,' he said quietly. 'See the way they're looking at each other?' He smiled affably. 'I don't think it will be too long before Alexander pops the question. I mean, it's a foregone conclusion – they've been close all their lives and they've spent so much time together, on and off – it would be a pair well matched. A marriage made in heaven!'

Elizabeth nodded, her head on one side. 'Yes, all that is true, Jacob,' she said, 'but Alexander is still in the middle of his studies. It will be some time before he can support a wife and children.'

Jacob tried not to laugh out loud. 'Good heavens, Elizabeth!' he said. 'The dowry Honora will take with her will be sufficient to last them for years! And I can't see Randolph holding back with the cash. Money's got nothing to do with it. Nothing!'

Elizabeth wasn't convinced. 'The thing is, Jacob, I can see a real difference, a real change, in Alexander since he's come home,' she said slowly. 'I'm afraid it may not turn out as we have always hoped it would be for them.'

Jacob sat back, startled. 'What do you mean when you say that you think Alexander is different? He seems exactly the same to me! But of course he may have changed a *little* bit – just look what he's gone through! It must have been enough to drive a man completely mad. No wonder if he might seem a little bit "different". But that will all come right, you wait and see.'

Jacob poured more wine into his wife's glass. 'Don't you worry, my dear,' he said. 'I am pretty certain that it won't be too long before you've got a big society wedding to arrange, because I know that Alexander will do what's expected of him.' Jacob drained his own glass. 'Alexander will always do the right thing,' he said. 'You can depend on that, my dear.'

Chapter 18

December 1919

To Angelina, and to all the nurses, it felt as if they had exchanged one battlefront for another as the influenza pandemic continued to rage. As the last of the remaining soldiers were being demobilised, it was obvious that they – as many before them – were bringing back infections from the trenches for which there seemed little remedy. Sepsis, another deadly disease, had joined influenza in wiping out hundreds of the population within a matter of weeks, or even days.

The government did what it could, ordering the temporary closure of theatres and restaurants. Church halls and meeting places followed suit, and the permanent cleaning of streets with chemicals added to the sense of panic. Was the entire country to be annihilated? At one point it was thought that smoking might be a deterrent to infection, and Randolph Garfield gave away thousands of free cigarettes in an effort to stem the tide.

Since their return, Angelina had been working on the women's medical ward, while Jane had had to suspend her training and return home to care for her parents, both of whom had developed serious health issues.

147

'Don't worry, I'll be coming back,' she'd declared to Angelina. 'But I can hardly let my parents cope with their problems on their own, can I?' Angelina had smiled. Despite all she'd said about having felt emotionally neglected as a child, Jane had a heart of gold.

One evening, on her way to the canteen before she started her night shift Angelina bumped into Norma. Since the two were no longer sharing a room, they'd hardly had the chance for a proper chat, and Norma said, 'Are you going to the canteen? I've got an hour before my next theatre duty so I'll come with you.' She caught Angelina's arm. 'Can you bear to talk about everything that happened over there? I mean I can only hazard a guess at what you all went through, but—'

Angelina interrupted. 'I'm sure you've got a pretty good idea, Norma, but… if you don't mind, I'd rather not go into it.'

They sat down at a table in the corner, and Angelina said, 'By the way, you may be flattered to know that I thought of you a lot when I was over there because it was thanks to you that I became hooked on theatre work. I had watched all those operations here, like you suggested, and read everything I could get my hands on, so when they were calling for a theatre nurse I volunteered – and I was taken up straightaway!' Angelina made a face. 'Mind you, they didn't have much choice because they were desperate. BHonestly, thinking about it I don't know how I had the cheek, but I must have done all right because they kept calling out for me.'

Norma raised her eyes. 'Well done you, Angelina,' she said slowly. 'Experience is the best teacher as we all know. You will obviously have learned a great deal.'

They ordered what they wanted to eat and drink and Angelina said, 'You must have been in on hundreds of operations now, Norma. Do you ever get tired of it, and would rather switch to something else?'

'Nope,' Norma said cheerfully. 'But I will let you into my

little secret, Angelina.' She paused. 'I've got a new boyfriend, one of the surgeons I've been working with. We've been going out for six months now and he's absolutely gorgeous – even when he's wielding a knife!'

Angelina clapped her hands. 'Oh Norma! How exciting! Have you told anybody?'

'Only you,' Norma said. 'We're keeping it quiet in case it all goes wrong – but I don't think it will.' She paused. 'It's funny, but I have a gut instinct that we are meant to be together... for always. I mean he is not only handsome, he's kind and thoughtful, and when we're talking he doesn't drop his gaze, or look away.' She smiled quickly. 'It's as if I'm the only person in the world that he's interested in. Does that sound silly to you?'

Angelina gazed into the far distance. 'No, it doesn't sound silly at all,' she said quietly.

After they'd finished eating they stood up to leave. 'By the way – there was an announcement in The Times this week about the son of your Mr Garfield.' Norma said. She had always known that Angelina had been a Garfield orphan.

Angelina looked up, startled. 'Really? What – what did it say?'

'That Miss Honora Mason and Mr Alexander Garfield have become engaged to be married, that's all,' Norma said. 'See – love is in the air!'

*

Three days later, on her forty-eight-hour pass, Angelina made her way to the orphanage to see Miss Kingston. Ever since she'd heard the news about Alexander's engagement, Angelina had been so depressed she could barely concentrate on her duties, and she knew that going 'home' for a few hours and talking to the superintendent would help put things into perspective. Of course she was being stupid, because Angelina had known all along that those two would get married. They were perfect for each other, both coming from prestigious families and backgrounds. But now that it was actually to become fact, it felt to Angelina as if she had been punched a blow from which she would never recover.

She tried to console herself. Surely she wouldn't be feeling this bad if fate – and war – hadn't thrown them together on that battlefront, and if Alexander hadn't kissed her and held her close and whispered sweet things into her ear…? Could she be blamed for believing, even for a second, that he had meant it, and that he really wanted her in that way? Or that, by some miracle she, and not Honora Mason, would one day be forever at his side?

She arrived at the orphanage, and, unusually, Miss Jones answered the door, her face breaking into a huge smile when she saw Angelina.

'My dear Angelina!' Maria Jones exclaimed, automatically pulling Angelina to her and giving her a hug. 'What a nice surprise! We don't see nearly enough of you!'

'Hullo Miss Jones,' Angelina said. 'Mrs Marshall not here today?'

'No, she's having a couple of days off because her husband is having one of his funny spells,' Maria said She looked more closely at Angelina. 'Are *you* all right, dear? You do look very pale.'

Angelina smiled. I'm fine, thanks, just rather tired because I've been on nights and now I'm trying to adjust to normal life again. Night duty does turn life upside down,' she added.

Emma Kingston appeared from her study. 'Oh lovely!' she said. 'An unexpected visit from one of our children!' She glanced at Miss Jones. 'Would you arrange coffee for us, Miss Jones?'

After they had exchanged the usual pleasantries, the super-intendent said, 'Now then, tell me all the news. Are you being worked off your feet as usual?' She sighed briefly. 'This pandemic is the last thing you must all have needed.'

Angelina nodded. 'It isn't easy,' she said, 'but we're doing our best.' She paused, looking away, her face so full of pain, that Emma Kingston leaned forward and touched Angelina's arm.

150

'What is it, dear?' she said. 'Is something wrong?' It was obvious that Angelina was not her usual, engaging self.

Angelina didn't smile. 'No, Miss Kingston, there's nothing wrong... not at work, I mean...'

'What then?' the superintendent asked, a trace of anxiety in her tone. This was not like Angelina Green, the unstoppable, ever optimistic young woman. 'What's troubling you, dear?'

The last thing Angelina wanted was sympathy, but she managed to hold back a sob in her throat. Fortunately, Miss Jones arrived then with their drinks, breaking the tension, and whether it was the warming coffee, or just being in Miss Kingston's presence, Angelina knew she was going to spill her anguish. She put down her cup and tried to speak normally.

'I've just heard that... that Mr Alexander is engaged to be married,' she said, and Emma Kingston nodded.

'Yes – it was in The Times, I believe,' she said, 'though when Mr Garfield looked in here last week he didn't mention it. Though why should he? It's hardly our business, is it?'

Angelina couldn't hold it in any longer, and she clasped her hands together tightly. 'Mr Alexander and I – we met each other, Miss Kingston, while we were over there,' Angelina whispered. She waited for a long moment before going on. 'He was in uniform and I was on duty and he saw me first – and he just called out my name and it was like a beautiful dream to be standing there together amongst all that unbelievable chaos.'

Angelina didn't go on, because she could not bring herself to explain any further. How could she possibly describe how she had been held and kissed and hugged. Would Miss Kingston even believe her? Believe that the son of the philanthropist owner of the Garfield would behave like that with her, Angelina Green, an abandoned orphan, a nobody?

After a few moments' silence, Emma Kingston said softly, 'And were you able to enjoy any time together before he went away again? Was there a chance to really talk to each other?'

Angelina nodded miserably. 'Yes. We had two hours, two whole hours,' she said. 'And if the world could have stopped turning at that moment, and fixed us there for ever, I would have been happier than I can possibly say.'

The superintendent leaned forward to pour them both another coffee, her face a picture of understanding and sympathy. She didn't need to hear any more from Angelina. From a very young child, Angelina had been besotted with Alexander Garfield – and in fairness to her, he had always treated her with masculine charm. Angelina's feelings had clearly never wavered, but... why did there always have to be a 'but'...?

'I don't think I've ever told anyone of my own experience when I was young,' Emma Kingston said quietly, 'but this might be the right opportunity to share something with you, Angelina.'

Angelina looked up quickly. Miss Kingston had always been a very private person. No one had any real knowledge of her life before the orphanage.

'When I was about your age,' Emma Kingston said slowly, 'I was governess to three small children – their mother had died just a few months before.' Emma sipped her coffee. 'They were a rich family, and the children's father took a great interest in their wellbeing, and how I was doing my job. It was such a happy arrangement and the children seemed to love me – as I certainly loved them.' The superintendent paused, smiling sadly at her own memories. 'The younger one sometimes called me "Mummy" by mistake, which always sent a shiver down my spine.'

Angelina was engrossed in what she was hearing. How was this going to end?

'On the first anniversary of his wife's death,' Emma Kingston said, 'my employer came to the nursery as usual – to say goodnight to the children – and presently we sat together in the firelight, just talking. He was an important businessman and sometimes, when he'd had a really long day, he seemed to like being there with me. Just the two of us.'

After another long silence, Emma Kingston said slowly, 'That night, the most unbelievable, the most unexpected thing took place, that afterwards I asked myself if it really had happened.' Emma Kingston's voice dropped to almost a whisper. 'He drew me into his arms... and then he kissed me. On the lips, I mean, fully on the lips. It was my first – my only – experience of such a thing and I'd had no instruction. But I understood what it meant, oh yes, and I responded. Quite readily.' She smiled. 'He was a very handsome man, and I was completely overwhelmed.'

The superintendent drew in a deep breath. 'It's strange that when the time comes, nature prepares us for all eventualities.'

Angelina hardly knew what to do or say. This news was the private property of a very private person, and she, Angelina, was being trusted with it. 'And... afterwards?' she said quietly.

'I'm afraid there was no afterwards,' Emma Kingston said. 'I had been stupid enough to believe that I was being loved, and wanted, and that I would become those children's mother. That brief closeness, that one kiss, had been enough to make me hope that I had a future with that family... with that man.' Her voice trailed off for a moment.

'Instead of which, the occasion was never referred to again and my employer re-married a woman in his own class. She was actually his cousin,' the superintendent added, 'and far more suitable a person to accompany him on his many important appointments. I had merely been a momentary stop-gap in his emotional life, something passing and pointless.'

Emma Kingston finished her coffee and straightened up. 'Never mind, it didn't take me too long to accept what I could not change, Angelina, and although I had longed for children of my own, it was not to be.' She smiled brightly. 'So I comforted myself in looking after other people's – and I have been a happy woman, my dear, a very happy woman. Now that I can look back on it, I do believe that it had all been for the best.'

Her mind trying to take in all that she'd heard, presently

153

Angelina made her goodbyes and was about to leave when Maria Jones appeared holding a small box of cakes.

'Some little treats for you and Ruby,' Maria Jones said, following her to the main door.

Just then the priest arrived. 'Good afternoon ladies,' he said, bowing extravagantly, and in spite of all Angelina had hear and her own distress, she wanted to giggle.

'Did you want something, Father?' Maria Jones said innocently, 'I mean, were you looking for someone?'

He didn't hesitate. 'Yes – I know the children have finished school for the day, but I wondered if Sister Bernadette was still in the school room,' he said casually. 'I'll just pop in and take a look around.'

After he'd gone, Maria Jones rolled her eyes at Angelina. 'He's a weird one,' she said, 'always haunting the place like a big black ghost! You never know when he's going to turn up! And you wouldn't want to hear Mrs Haines's opinion of him!'

*

After Angelina had left, Emma Kingston sat with her elbows on the desk and rested her head in her hands. Having opened her sacred box of memories just now had left her feeling sad, and a little depressed. Which was not like Emma Kingston. She seldom, if ever, felt low.

But this had been an unusual occasion on which she could do nothing to help Angelina, and that was what was depressing. In an effort to ally herself with Angelina, she had confided in her little orphan, told her things that had not been spoken of or barely thought about for more than thirty years. But it hadn't helped. It hadn't helped her, Emma Kingston, and neither had it been any use to Angelina, because they both knew there could be no happy ending. It seemed that where Alexander Garfield was concerned the die was cast, his future sealed.

And that future could never include Angelina.

Emma went across to the window and stared outside. It was almost Christmas, a time to be jolly – in spite of the country's present woes.

Then a smile played on her lips as she thought back to all the Christmases they'd enjoyed at Garfield. She thought of her orphan children, so many of whom had done well in their lives since leaving the shelter of the orphanage. Most held down good jobs to support themselves, quite a few of the girls had gone into nursery nursing or had secured desk jobs in the town. Over the years some of the boys had been taken on by Jacob Mason, who'd been civil enough to compliment the superintendent on their ability and willingness to learn. Two of them had recently been accepted by Rolls Royce as trainees, which was really something.

Emma's eyes clouded for a second. There had been sad news of several of her boys losing their lives on the Front during the war – but that had been inevitable. They had been doing their duty to the best of their ability, which is all that should be expected of anyone. But to give your life for your country was the ultimate sacrifice.

The superintendent wiped her eyes briefly. Even though she had prayed for them every night, it was hopeless to think that all her children could have been saved from an untimely death on the battlefield. But she would always be proud of each and every one of them.

And what of Ruby Lane? The damaged, speechless child who, it had been thought, would probably end her days in an asylum? Ruby Lane had blossomed and blossomed! Maria Jones – who had always kept an eye on the youngster – had been told by the owner of the hairdressing salon that a bright future awaited. That Ruby had natural flair and ability and could go far if she so wished.

Emma Kingston drew in a deep breath of gratitude. Who would ever have thought that?

But of course, that was largely thanks to Angelina Green. Their shoebox baby, who was herself now destined for great things in the nursing profession. She alone had somehow managed to bring little Ruby back to some kind of normality, to give her a chance of life.

The superintendent halted in her own thoughts. What a testimony to take with you for the rest of your life – that you might have saved another human being from an unspeakable future…

And wasn't that what she, Emma Kingston, had been doing all her life? She might now, at this very moment, have been grandmother to the babies of those three children she had loved and cared for all that time ago. She might even have had her own babies, if fate had allowed it, and be living in luxury with her handsome employer.

But instead, she had loved and cared for hundreds of little ones who'd had a wretched start in life. Hundreds! What a privilege.

Emma Kingston smiled happily to herself.

She wouldn't change a single thing.

Chapter 19

March 1920

Angelina tapped on the almoner's door and went in, knowing that what she was about to be told would either make her day or ruin it. The day that she had been working towards for so long. Had she passed her Finals? Was she now a fully qualified registered nurse? Had all those lectures, all that practical, often tortuous, experience, been enough?

Or must she wait another year and do better next time?

The almoner looked up. 'Come and sit down, Angelina,' Miss Day said. 'I am not going to keep you in suspense – congratulations my dear!' She smiled broadly. 'You have passed with flying colours – as we knew you would! All of us at St Thomas's are extremely proud of you!'

Angelina had imagined how she might feel at this moment. Would she burst into tears, or whoop with delight, or gabble some silly words that said there must be some mistake in the marking? She did none of those things, only felt enormous relief that she could now get on with the next part of her life.

'Thank you, Miss Day,' she said quietly, then, without hesitation, she added – 'I wonder if you would do me a favour?'

The almoner raised her eyebrows. 'If it is within my province then I will with pleasure,' she said. 'What do you have in mind?'

'I would like my name to be put forward to enter medical school,' Angelina said. 'Because I wish to train to be a doctor, and finally, perhaps, to become a consultant orthopaedic surgeon.'

Miss Day barely suppressed a smile, remembering the day this youngster had sat here wishing to enter the nurses' training school, her youthful ambition and determination to achieve her aim impossible to deny. And how well Nurse Angelina Green had proved her worth! A tribute to human endeavour against all the odds.

The almoner gazed across. 'You do realise you would be facing a very long period of training,' she said. 'In total it would amount to eight or nine years – or even longer. Would you be ready to submit your whole life to that pressure and dedication?' She paused. 'You have been through a very tough few years, Angelina – don't you feel ready for a break, a little time to sit back for a while?'

'No, I don't feel ready for that at all, Miss Day,' Angelina said, leaning forward earnestly. 'This is not something I've only just thought about,' she said. 'It's been in my mind for several years, especially since I was on the front line. I saw the amazing things the surgeons were able to do… when sometimes it felt that there was no hope. It was like seeing miracles taking place and I was there, watching, *assisting*! I was part of all that and I thought, I can do this! I can see how it's done! And however long it takes, I am determined to get there if they will admit me and train me.' Angelina paused for breath. 'The medical world is my whole world, Miss Day. There will never be anything else and I do not want anything else.'

The almoner's eyes moistened. It was impossible not to be swept along by this young woman's genuine enthusiasm.

She stood up. 'Your contract with us will end in July,' she said briskly, 'so you would be available to begin elsewhere in September. It may be possible for you to join the medical intake at, say, UCL or Guy's.' She smiled. 'I'll do my best for you, Angelina, make the right enquiries and speak to the right people – but I am afraid Matron will not be very pleased if you do depart. We have only just got used to having you back home with us again!'

Angelina felt her face flush with excitement. Miss Day had taken her seriously.

Angelina Green would soon be on the next step of her ladder.

May 1920

Angelina finished making their egg and watercress sandwiches – Ruby's favourite Saturday teatime meal – and reached for the tin that held their precious cakes. Removing the lid, she saw that another dozen had been added: tiny orange butterfly sponges, a speciality of Mrs Haines's. Angelina smiled to herself. It seemed that Miss Jones regularly found some excuse to pop into their house and leave a parcel containing sweet meats of one kind or another, so their tin was never empty for long.

It was five-thirty. Ruby would be home soon because the last appointment at the salon was always at four o'clock on Saturdays. And as this was Angelina's weekend off, the two girls had decided to go into town later to see a film, or just to browse the shops. Because of Angelina's shifts, they didn't often have the chance to be together like this, and they were both looking forward to it.

With the table set for their tea, Angelina turned one of the chairs to face the window, then sat down and gazed out. It was a fine evening with summer beckoning, and the exciting prospect of September and what would follow on after that, made her heart rush with anticipation. After several interviews, they had accepted her application at UCL, and now all she wanted to do was to get started, to get on with it! When she had told Miss

Kingston the news, the superintendent had been almost speechless with amazement.

'From the moment you arrived here, Angelina,' she'd said, 'we all knew you would go far. But really – I did not imagine the heights you were going to achieve. You are a credit to yourself and to us, my dear, living proof that whatever one's beginnings, nothing is impossible if you work hard and are determined.' She had hugged Angelina to her tightly. 'I cannot wait to tell Miss Jones your news, because she is so proud of you and Ruby. She thinks you are such brave and clever little girls – and she is right!'

But above all the euphoria regarding her future, it was with some relief that Angelina could say that she was happy inside herself once more. She had faced up to her demon and sent it packing, promising herself that she would never again let her heart rule her head, never again wish or hope for the impossible, the unobtainable. She shook her head, irritated at her own thoughts. She must have been completely mad to have thought that she could mean anything to Alexander Garfield. Mad, stupid, and infantile – yes, that's what she had been – infantile! She'd had a childish dream that one day he would love her as she loved him, but dreams were just that – dreams. They were not reality.

Angelina lowered her eyes, tracing the pattern on the tablecloth with her forefinger thoughtfully. But had she been entirely to blame in all this? Wasn't there someone else in this hopeless equation?

Well, yes! Yes! What had taken place in that field in France had been no dream, it had been reality! With Alexander's arms around her so closely they'd been like one person, with his lips almost devouring hers, over and over, with him saying, 'Don't be sorry because I'm not a bit sorry.' That had been reality!

Despite all her best intentions, Angelina's shoulders drooped. What had that all been about? Had Alexander completely forgotten about it, as if it had never happened? Had he forgotten those two hours they'd spent together with his hand holding hers, refusing to let it go? For the first time in their lives they had talked as two friends, as equals, not just discussing the present situation but exchanging views and opinions about everything under the sun, making each other laugh about little things they remembered when Alexander had come to the orphanage with his father.

For Angelina, those two hours had been a blissful break from the horror and distress all around, and being there, just the two of them, had felt absolutely right, absolutely perfect.

And she'd remembered not to call him 'Mr Alexander' He had been just Alexander. Her long-time friend.

Angelina thought about what Miss Kingston had told her of her own experience, and not for the first time, Angelina felt angry. Angry at the injustice of the superintendent's situation, and of her own, too. It was not fair! Why did a man – any man – play games with the emotional feelings of a woman, and then calmly walk away? Didn't they realise how it hurt? How it stung?

Angelina shook herself angrily and stood up. That demon *would* keep reappearing! But she must take Miss Kingston's advice and forget all that had happened and look to the future. And that was exactly what Nurse Angelina Green – one day, hopefully, to become Dr Green and eventually *Miss Green*, in surgeon's language – was going to do. Forget the past and fix her eyes on the future.

Could she do that, honestly? Angelina pursed her lips. It was going to be hard, but, as usual, she would do her best.

*

It was nearly seven o'clock before Ruby came home, breathless from having run all the way.

'Sorry I'm late!' she exclaimed, 'but just before we closed Mr Walker and Robert called in, and we all just stood there, chatting.' Ruby went across to the sink to wash her hands before going on excitedly. 'You'll never guess, Angelina, but I've been asked to go to a function with them – with the family!'

Angelina raised her eyes.

'Really? What sort of function?'

'They explained that it's to do with the Masons… a sort of gentlemen's club or 'Lodge' to which Mr Walker belongs, and every year they hold a Ladies' Night which means that members can invite their wives and families.' Ruby dried her hands and went across to the table to join Angelina who was pouring their tea. 'Anyway, the thing is, Robert doesn't have a partner to go with him, and they wondered whether I might like to make up the foursome.' Ruby sat down and leaned her elbows on the table. 'Honestly, Angelina, I couldn't believe they would want me… I mean Robert must have plenty of friends at his college that he could ask but Mrs Walker kept insisting that Robert would prefer me to sit beside him, that we know each other very well now – because we never stop chatting whenever he calls in at the salon. She said there would be a very nice meal, and dancing afterwards! And I said the only dance I could do was the waltz because we used to do that in the playroom sometimes… do you remember, Angelina? When we were all messing about?'

'I remember, Ruby,' Angelina said.

'The thing that's worrying me is what I am going to wear,' Ruby went on. 'Mrs Walker explained that the ladies are usually in long frocks, but that it wouldn't matter if I wore short. She said that anything simple and summery would do, and Mr Walker said he thought I would look lovely if I just wore a sack!' Ruby sat back and clasped her hands together. 'All this has made me feel that I've been hit by a whirlwind, Angelina! Why would they invite *me* – I mean I'm just a member of their staff. No one special…'

Angelina leaned across and squeezed Ruby's hand. 'But you are someone special, Ruby,' she said, 'and you always have been. That is why Mrs Walker took you on.' Angelina paused. 'And

Robert must think you are special, or he wouldn't have wanted you as his partner.'

Ruby dropped her gaze. 'Well, it is true that Robert seems to like me,' she said quietly. 'I've never bothered to tell you before, but on Valentine's Day he gave me a rose. I didn't think too much of it because Mr Walker gave Mrs Walker one as well, but when Robert gave me mine he held my hand tightly and wouldn't let it go!' Ruby took a deep breath. 'Do you think I'm being silly, Angelina, because I really, really, like him. From the moment I set eyes on him I knew he was someone I would love being with. Am I being stupid?'

'Of course you aren't being stupid,' Angelina said slowly 'Now, when is this function to take place?'

'On the first Saturday of next month.'

'Good. That gives us three weeks to find you a dress.' Angelina said briskly. 'There's no time like the present, so we start tonight! As soon as we've had tea, we'll go into town and look in all the windows for some ideas. The market always has nice material in stock so between us we'll produce something that will make Robert proud to show you off.' Angelina smiled. 'At least you don't have to find a good hairdresser!'

Dear Miss Jones,

I hope you won't think me impertinent, but I have a great favour to ask. Ruby has been invited by her employers to accompany them to a very special party, and she has nothing suitable to wear. The occasion calls for a long dress, and of course Ruby does not have one. At first, I thought she and I could make one between us, but you know, more than anyone, that our needlework lessons at the orphanage did not run to cutting out from a long length of material – and then making a dress to fit in all the right places! Would you do it for us – for Ruby? We have enough money to buy quite a nice material – we've already looked in the market – and the pattern would only need to be a simple one. All we need is your magic needle, if you have the time.

Ruby and I would quite understand if you are too busy.

The party is to take place in just under three weeks.

Yours sincerely,

Angelina

Chapter 20

July 1920

Senior Nurse Green slowly accompanied the doctor as he visited each patient in the women's medical ward. It was a routine procedure which took place a couple of times a week, its purpose to examine the notes at the foot of each bed, and to discuss the progress, or otherwise, of each woman.

As always, Angelina was able to answer any query the doctor might have with no problem – she had been in charge of this ward since her return from the Front, and knew all her patients and their specific needs without having to continually refer to their records. As it had been with her soldiers, while the sick were in her care, they were her family.

The doctor finished his rounds and left the ward, and Angelina returned to her desk. As she sat there in the quiet, immaculately hygienic surroundings, she could not stop her mind from returning to France... to the noise... to the mud and squalor... to the filth... the terror. How had she come through all that, relatively unscathed? And why hadn't Heather come home with them?

Angelina stopped what she was doing for a moment, and

put down her pen, aware that among all those thoughts was a more surprising one. She was missing those awful days, actually missing them. How could that possibly be? To get away from all that, and come home safe and sound had been everyone's overriding wish, yet looking back on it, she realised what a wonderful time, what a wonderful experience it had been. All the friends she'd made – not necessarily close friends, but friends united in a common purpose, looking out for each other, looking after each other. It had been teamwork to a degree she would surely never again experience, and Angelina was grateful. She had learned so much about others, and so much about herself. In its own strange way, being there fighting a war alongside her fellow nurses had been a privilege, and she would never forget a single bit of it.

Just then, one of the orderlies arrived with details of an urgent case about to be admitted from Accident & Emergency, and glancing down at the papers she'd been given, Angelina frowned. Someone called Valentina Marshall was about to occupy the only vacant bed on the ward – surely this had to be Mrs Marshall from the orphanage? Once, when Angelina had been in the kitchen she'd overheard Mrs Marshall reveal her unusual Christian name to Mrs Haines – who'd received the information with a raised eyebrow. But Angelina he remembered being told that Mrs Marshall had had some time off over the last few months because she hadn't been feeling well.

It was Mrs Marshall, but when she was wheeled in on the trolley it took Angelina by surprise. The woman looked gaunt and grey and so much older than she used to look. Angelina went over to speak to her.

'Hello Mrs Marshall,' Angelina said quietly. 'Now, what have you been doing to yourself may I ask?'

Mrs Marshall smiled faintly, grasping Angelina's hand. 'Oh Angelina,' she said, 'I never expected to have to come to hospital… I mean, I'm never ill. You know that. But I can't get rid of this wretched cough and I've been finding it difficult to breathe – especially at night.'

As if to prove the point, she began wheezing and coughing, and it was obvious that she was in considerable pain.

Angelina squeezed her hand sympathetically. 'Don't worry, you've come to the right place,' she said. 'We'll soon make you more comfy.'

Without looking at Angelina, Mrs Marshall said, 'I had no idea they'd be keeping me in overnight. I thought it would be a quick examination downstairs and then I'd be given some tablets to take home with me.' She paused. 'But if I had to stay, I was hoping I'd be on your ward, Angelina.'

Angelina smiled at that. After all, she had never been Mrs Marshall's favourite child. Just then, the emergency doctor arrived and Angelina went over to the desk with him for a discussion about their new patient.

'I'm afraid it does look like another TB case,' the doctor said, 'rather than the dreaded flu – which was our first thought. We shall have to wait for the X-rays.'

Angelina nodded. 'So, obviously, Mrs Marshall needs to go straight into the isolation side ward? And luckily here is a bed available,' Angelina added.

'Good – thanks.' As he turned to leave, the doctor said, 'May I wish you good luck, Nurse Green? In your next venture I mean.' Angelina had become very well-known at St Thomas's. Everyone knew she was leaving, and everyone knew she had been one of the heroic front line nurses.

Angelina smiled quickly. 'Thanks – I'm looking forward to it.'

*

Angelina's shift was to finish at nine o'clock, and she wasn't due back on the ward until midday tomorrow, so she was going to spend the night in her own bed. This was quite a treat, especially

167

as it gave her and Ruby the chance to go on talking, however late it was, before they finally fell asleep. Neither of them were ever short of anecdotes about their working day, and Ruby's experiences in the salon were always worth hearing about. She had a funny way of mimicking some of their clients, and to Angelina it seemed a happy, breezy, way of earning a living.

It was eight o'clock – one hour to go before her relief took over – and Angelina sat back and stretched her arms above her head. The last hour was always the longest.

The ward was quiet, all the medications had been administered, and most of the patients were asleep. And as Angelina's thoughts wandered, she remembered again how beautiful Ruby had looked in the dress which Miss Jones had made for her.

The day after Angelina's letter had arrived at the orphanage, Miss Jones had come to the house, full of ideas and enthusiasm. It had only been Ruby there at the time, but Ruby had described the visit in detail.

'Of course I am not too busy to make either of you a dress!' Miss Jones had exclaimed. 'I shall make you look like a princess, Ruby. Leave it to me!'

And when the great day arrived and Ruby had put on the dress and presented her appearance for Angelina's inspection, Angelina – only just having come home from work – had been almost bowled over.

The dress was a simple, full-length creation in a soft lavender-coloured silky material, its scooped neckline showing off Ruby's fine skin, its dropped waistline, with a large bow at the hip, accentuating her graceful figure. Ruby had trained most of her unruly fair curls to remain firmly clipped to the top of her head, while allowing just one or two fronds to stray prettily either side of her face.

For a few seconds, Angelina had remained speechless. Miss Jones had been as good as her word. Little Ruby Lane did indeed look like a princess.

When Robert Walker had arrived at their door to escort Ruby to the car waiting outside, Angelina had thought she was watching a fairy tale take place. Robert, a tall, dark-haired young man was wearing a dinner jacket, white shirt and black bow tie, and as he'd looked at Ruby it was obvious that he was enchanted. As well he might be, Angelina had thought. Miss Jones had woven another of her magic spells.

Thinking about that now, Angelina was ashamed to admit that, at the time, she had been envious of Ruby. Really envious. Because she had wished that it was she going to that party – with Alexander – and that Alexander had been looking down at her in the way in which Robert Walker had gazed at Ruby. He had taken her hand straightaway, and held it, like Angelina remembered hers being held. Then, and now, it had seemed like a physical statement of ownership, and it was obvious that Ruby had been starry-eyed as she'd looked up at Robert.

Now, Angelina sighed at all her memories. Whatever else life might give you, why was there always one more thing that you wanted? She had yearned to be a nurse, and she was one, fully qualified. She'd wanted to go much further in her medical career, and that wish, too, was being granted. Yet there was still one more thing she longed for.

It was to be with the one person she had always loved. And would, for the rest of her life.

Yet that was where her luck had run out. She could never be Alexander Garfield's wife. It had been written in the stars.

Just before her relief arrived to take over, Angelina went into the isolation ward to check on her four patients. Three of them were sleeping fitfully, but Mrs Marshall appeared to be awake, and she smiled faintly as Angelina approached.

'I don't think those tablets you gave me are working, Angelina,' Mrs Marshall whispered. 'Can I have some more?'

'I'm afraid not,' Angelina replied softly, 'but the next round of medication is due in an hour.' She paused. 'Try and relax – you will start to feel better in a day or two.' Angelina sighed inwardly. She hoped Mrs Marshall hadn't left it too late before seeking help.

After a moment, Angelina said, 'Is someone looking after your husband while you're here, Mrs Marshall?'

Mrs Marshall's expression didn't waver. 'No. I told him he could look after himself for a change,' she said. 'Anyway, he's not my husband. I've never been married.'

'Really?' Angelina was very surprised at this unexpected news. 'But why…?

Mrs Marshall shook her head wearily. 'Oh, well, you are far more respected if you are a married woman,' she said. 'It somehow places you on a higher level than if you are a spinster.' She paused before going on. 'So I decided that I would tell everyone my brother was my husband, and I've been looking after him since our mother died. We never knew our father, and I was 10 years old when I was given the task of bringing up my 5-year-old brother. And he's never gone to school because he's got mental problems.'

Angelina didn't want to believe this sad story. Poor Mrs Marshall, poor short-tempered Mrs Marshall. Who could blame her if she was always cross?

Angelina cleared her throat. 'So – is your brother capable of looking after himself?' she asked gently.

'Oh yes, he can do the essentials,' Mrs Marshall said. 'I've taught him that much. And my neighbour next door will look in to make sure he hasn't done anything silly. But he's a lazy beggar. It'll do him good to stand on his own feet for a change.'

Angelina hardly knew what to say to all this, but Mrs Marshall hadn't finished.

'I want to say something else while I'm about it, Angelina,' she said, 'and it's to explain why I always seemed to pick on you when you were a child.'

'Oh, don't worry about that!' Angelina said. 'That's all in the past!'

'It was because I was so envious of you,' Mrs Marshall went on, determined to have her say, Angelina interrupted.

170

'Envious of me, Mrs Marshall?' she said. 'Why would you possibly be envious of me?'

'Because you were a Garfield orphan. I would love to have been brought up in the Garfield, or in any orphanage, to be looked after in comfort and safety.' She sighed deeply. 'But it wasn't only that. I was one of the first to see you when you... when you arrived... and it seemed as if a lucky star shone above your head. You were the most beautiful baby I had ever set eyes on, and everyone doted on you from the very beginning, giving you the sort of attention that I've never had in my life. As you grew up, it seemed that you could do nothing wrong. You were always clever and bright... you've been *lucky*, Angelina. Something I have never been,' Mrs Marshall added. 'And I am ashamed to admit that to be nasty and unkind to you gave me pleasure. Isn't that horrible? But it seemed like fair justice that I could make you unhappy now and then... as if I was saying, there, see what it feels like to be miserable.'

Mrs Marshall tried to reach her drink on the table beside her, and Angelina immediately leaned over to get it for her. 'Please don't tire yourself, Mrs Marshall,' she said. 'Here – let me plump up your pillow.'

'I just want to hear you say that you forgive me, Angelina,' Mrs Marshall said. 'Every time I made it difficult for you, especially when, you know, I spilt all that food on the floor and blamed you for it – I always felt sorry afterwards. But it was like a devil inside me, a devil I had no control over.'

Angelina smiled down at her kindly. 'Mrs Marshall, you don't need my forgiveness, you need my understanding. And I do understand it, I understand everything. You have had a very difficult, unenviable life, while I have been blessed. And you have worked so hard to support yourself and your brother, and you are tireless at the orphanage. What would Miss Kingston do without you?'

'The orphanage – even before it was the Garfield – has been

171

my salvation,' Mrs Marshall said simply. 'Even though I did not have its succour and comfort as a child, for the last thirty years it has been where I am most happy and content. I would have wanted to die if Mr Garfield hadn't saved us.'

'Well, he did, didn't he, so that's a lovely part of the story,' Angelina said, turning to leave the ward. As she went, Mrs Marshall said, 'It must be lovely to be you, Angelina, to have everything you've ever wanted, I mean. With all your cleverness and success, there can't be a single thing that you still want... that you still wish for in life.'

Angelina turned back and smiled. 'Good night, Mrs Marshall. I will see you tomorrow,' she said softly.

Chapter 21

May 1921

'Angelina! Hang on a minute! I'm just coming!'

Angelina turned to see Dennis racing through the long corridor towards her, his white coat flying. He reached her side and automatically took her hand. 'I mislaid my notes,' he said, 'and stayed back to look for them.'

'Angelina smiled. Dennis was always losing things. 'Never mind – you could have copied up mine,' she said.

'What? And waste valuable time which could be spent far more pleasurably with my girlfriend?' Dennis retorted. 'Anyway, I found them, so the rest of the day is ours.'

The six young trainee doctors who'd all started their course in September had soon become close friends, usually meeting up in the canteen bar after their day shift for a coffee, or sometimes supper, before going home, or back to their quarters if they were on nights.

And it hadn't taken long for Dennis Edwards to stake his claim on Angelina. He was a tall, lanky, 25-year-old with a shock of thick fair hair, and an infectious laugh which usually set everyone else off as well. At their first seminar, he had edged himself along the row to sit in the spare seat next to Angelina, smiling down at her as he'd introduced himself.

'Hello. I'm Dennis Edwards,' he'd said cheerfully. 'Some may call me Dennis the Menace, but I'm perfectly harmless, I assure you.'

Angelina had smiled back immediately. 'I'm Angelina Green,' she'd said, 'from St Thomas's.'

He'd taken her hand. 'How do you do,' he'd said, straight-faced. Then they'd both started laughing, just as the lecturer arrived to take his place at the desk facing the row of eager-eyed trainees.

'Good morning all,' the lecturer had said, 'and welcome to the first day of the rest of your lives.' He had peered over his glasses. 'And may all the Gods go with you.'

There was a dutiful titter from the students, and Dennis had whispered into Angelina's ear, 'Can I buy you a drink later? Because from what he's just said I think we're going to need a pick-me-up from time to time.'

'All right – thanks,' Angelina had said, realising that she had just been asked out on a date. Her very first! At almost 21 years old she had never had a boyfriend, nor been asked out. Unlike Ruby, who was now Robert Walker's proper girlfriend – with his parents' delighted approval, so it seemed. Ruby had become one of the family, and she was thriving on it.

But that first day in her new career was where Angelina and Dennis had begun their relationship. He was a man so easy to like, and such fun to be with. But more often than not, they were part of a crowd, and this evening, as usual, they were all meeting in the canteen bar for a chat and a catch-up.

The two made their way downstairs, stopping briefly for Dennis to leave his white coat in his room, then he slipped his arm around Angelina's waist and pulled her in towards him. 'It's been a long few days, hasn't it,' he said. 'And I start on nights next week. I wonder which one of us is going to throw in the towel and change our minds about all this?'

174

Angelina would like to have said 'Not me!' but she didn't, because she didn't want to sound a self-satisfied goody-goody. But it was certainly true that they had all found the first nine months of their course intense and demanding. The days were long, the night shifts seeming even longer, and they were tested relentlessly by the duty doctors – who seemed to delight in humiliating the trainees by shooting questions at them in front of patients and expecting immediate and accurate answers.

During their times off, the young trainees were constantly studying to prepare themselves for the next round of interim exams. Most of them had not known such physical, as well as mental pressure before, but for Angelina it was nothing new. It seemed to her that her nursing life had inoculated her against the effects of fatigue – even if her maths and physics had required a little extra time and tuition.

Now, before they reached the canteen, Dennis said, 'We've both got the coming weekend off, haven't we? My parents would love to meet you, Angelina, because I've told them so much about you. My father served during the war, so you'd have lots to talk about.'

Angelina groaned inwardly. She had tried to put her experience in France to the very back of her mind, and had only touched briefly on the subject to the others, never giving any details. The thought of spending a long weekend going over the whole deadly business with complete strangers had no appeal at all.

She smiled up at Dennis. 'It's kind of your parents to invite me,' she said lightly, 'but can I let you know? It's just that I promised Ruby I'd spend a couple of hours with her in town on Saturday afternoon, because she's got some time off and needs help with buying a new pair of shoes.' Angelina crossed her fingers as she said that because, thanks to the Walkers, Ruby needed her less and less these days. In fact, it was very rarely – though the two girls still managed to make time for their long chats together whenever possible, and still shared all their secrets. But although Angelina really liked Dennis, she didn't want to be rushed into

175

an arrangement she might regret afterwards, and spending a weekend at his parents' house might put a rather different stamp on things. Angelina wasn't ready for that yet. Besides, she needed some time in the library to go over the physics paper she'd made such a mess of last week.

'Okay,' Dennis said easily. 'Anyway, when you've finished in town after shopping with Ruby, we could go after that.' He had met Ruby several times when he'd called for Angelina, and had taken to her immediately.

The others were already in the canteen bar when Angelina and Dennis arrived, and they automatically made room for them at the table. Tom, one of the older trainees, grinned over at them. 'What kept you, Dennis?' he said. 'We thought you'd stopped off for an illicit hour in bed! We know they've given you a new mattress!'

'No such luck unfortunately,' Dennis replied. 'Now, it's Thursday night and time for a proper bevy – and I'm buying! What would everyone like?'

'Well, that's very generous, Dennis,' Tom said heartily, 'and as I'm aware that it's your father's money you're spending I, for one, won't hold back! I'll have a Scotch on the rocks, and I bet Angelina could down a whole pint of vodka without stopping!'

There was a burst of laughter at that. Angelina seldom drank alcohol, and when she did it was a cider shandy which took her all the evening to finish.

The others all made their choices, and soon, with the long day over and the alcohol taking its effect, the noisy hilarity coming from the group as Dennis mimicked one of the more irritable senior doctors made other heads turn.

And then suddenly—

'Angelina?'

And there he was…

Alexander was at her side, looking down at her, and Angelina nearly fainted with amazement and complete shock! What on earth was he doing here?

176

With her heart missing a beat and, her hand flying to her throat, she half-stood.

'Alexander,' she began. 'What... why?'

He shrugged apologetically. 'Sorry if I'm an unpleasant surprise – but I need to speak to you, Angelina... It is something rather important,' he added.

Dennis stood up. 'Do introduce us, Angelina,' he said coolly, all his male instincts warning him that the new arrival suggested stiff competition. The man standing before them had immediately caught everyone's attention, his tall stature and innate good looks instantly attractive to every curious eye.

Alexander apologised to the group gazing up at him. 'My name is Alexander Garfield,' he said, 'and I am very sorry to intrude, but Angelina and I are, um, old friends from the past, and I have news which I know she would expect to be told. It is very serious, or I wouldn't have bothered you, Angelina,' he added, glancing at her.

Now Angelina's heart began racing. This must be something very serious, or why would he have turned up here at the hospital without warning?

'It's not Mr Randolph, is it? He is not ill? Or... is Miss Kingston all right?' Angelina's voice trembled with anxiety as she spoke.

Alexander shook his head quickly. 'No, my father and Miss Kingston are well, but – look Angelina, we can't talk here. Could we possibly meet some time over the weekend? If you are free, of course?'

Angelina's mind was reeling. What on *earth* was this all about? Whatever it was, there was surely nothing *she* could do about it! She hesitated before answering. 'Sorry,' she said, 'but Dennis—' she smiled and looked down at Dennis '—Dennis is my boyfriend – and his family have invited me to go with him to spend the weekend at the family home in the country. But I could meet you early next week if you like, say on Monday evening, Alexander?' she added.

Had she really said that, she asked herself? Had she really played hard to get when it would have been simple to see him as he'd asked? But it had been a natural reaction not to comply – after all, he had played havoc with her emotions in France, eventually leaving her bewildered and neglected. And that was hard to forgive, and to forget.

He stood back and nodded. 'Yes, that will be fine,' he said. 'Shall I come to your house… about eight o'clock?'

'Yes – Miss Kingston will give you my address.'

Alexander looked down at her and their eyes met.

'I know where you live,' he said briefly.

After he'd gone, Tom whistled through his teeth. 'Well, how many more male models do you know, Angelina?' he said.

'Yes,' one of the girls murmured. 'What a dish!'

Dennis was the only one who preferred to stay silent. Because, for some reason, Angelina had changed her mind about their weekend together. Now it seemed she was all for it. And the looks that had passed between those two had said a lot. There was something going on there, and he, Dennis Edwards, appeared to be a useful decoy for his girlfriend, for reasons, as yet, unknown.

Never mind, he was going to have his weekend away with the gorgeous Angelina after all, and that was good news indeed.

Though not such good news for Ruby, who'd have to choose her shoes all by herself.

Chapter 22

That same week, an event of some significance was to unfold at the Garfield Home for Children.

Across the road at the priory, the priest sat alone in the Confessional, that dark, sacred place of secrets and of restoration.

He sighed deeply. He had listened to three sad women this morning, all anxious to unload their guilt, but he was certain that they had truly repented and he had managed to reassure them that their sins were forgiven. And that they should now go in peace, and sin no more.

That was the point, of course. Go and sin no more.

For some reason, today would be the day that Laurence Dunn came to a decision. He was going to rid himself, once and for all, of the crushing weight of his own sin which he had shouldered alone for so many years. Well, he'd had no one else to tell, no one else who, by a few kind words, might have helped share his burden.

Sitting there quietly, with the consoling perfume of incense in his nostrils, he whispered, 'Bless me, Father, for I have sinned.'

Well, that was a beginning, but where now? Could he really find the words to explain that once you had tasted such pleasure it was impossible to stop wanting it, to stop tasting it? And that part of that pleasure was in avoiding detection? He had played a cat and mouse game for so many years it had become as essential to him as actually enjoying the fruits of his misdemeanour. It was true that he'd almost been caught out, several times, but had got better and better at his deviousness. Practice had made perfect...

But, at last, his mind was finally made up. It was going to stop and there would be no going back. He grimaced at that thought. Never to partake of that delight, that joy, that unhurried experience, ever again?

Well, yes. Today was going to be the day, and he knew he would feel better afterwards, once he'd accepted that it was all over.

Crossing his legs, he leaned back thoughtfully. He had learned over the years to be kind to himself from time to time, and he decided that he was going to ease the painful transition ahead by having just fifteen more minutes of human pleasure. Just once more. His mouth watered at the thought. And those fifteen minutes were going to happen this evening – if he could get away with it.

It was Friday. He'd heard all the confessions, had read the daily service, and had taken private Mass to two of the parish invalids, so the rest of the day was his. And now his tummy told him that it must be dinner time. He glanced at his watch. Yes, it was midday, and he often went across to the orphanage about now. He thought about that for a moment and decided that he would stay here today and have some bread and cheese in the priory kitchen for a change. It seemed a good idea to keep clear of the orphanage until later. To lie low.

At nine-thirty, drawing his cloak around him, the priest left the priory and walked the short distance over to the orphanage. There was little sound and it was still not quite dark, approaching nightfall adding to his sense of adventure.

With his own key he let himself into the building, shutting the door behind him noiselessly. Then he waited. The place was absolutely silent – well, all the children would be safely in bed and asleep now. The priest knew all the routines and procedures.

After all, he'd been part of the Garfield for so many years there was nothing you could tell Laurence Dunn about where and when the staff worked, what time the children had their meals, where they worked and played and slept. When it was quiet…

He made his way along the passage until he reached the kitchen – the nearest room to the back entrance of the building, which he always used. He went in quickly, shut the door, and stood with his back against it for a moment, waiting for his increased heart rate to settle down. Easy does it, he told himself.

The priest loved this kitchen. *Loved* it. If one could choose the place on earth where you would finally end your days, the orphanage kitchen would be his first choice.

It was a rectangular, high-ceilinged room with wide cupboards flanking every side, and with a huge, scrubbed wooden table in the centre where all the chopping and beating and mincing went on, and under which were a couple of stools. The two ovens were at the end, close to the deep sinks, and in the corner was the stove, its fire never allowed to go out. It was the original, trusty old stove which not only helped to heat all the water, but bathed the kitchen in a permanent and gentle warmth. And in front of the stove was Mrs Haines's own basket chair where, when time allowed, she would sit and relax.

But to Laurence Dunn, what gave this room its distinctive allure was the smell… the permanent lingering aroma of food recently prepared, the intoxicating perfume of baking bread, the mouthwatering scent of onions, or apples, or tomatoes marinating in some kind of potion which he could never give a name to. Taken altogether, the room personified a simple vision of heaven.

Happy that all was still and that his presence had not been discovered, he moved across to the longest cupboard above him on the wall and carefully slid the door across until all the contents were revealed.

And there they were. Rows and rows of jars holding preserved fruits and pickles, all neatly labelled. In the very front were the objects of the priest's desire – Mrs Haines's green tomato chutney. The queen of accompaniments to any meal! But the priest did not need a meal with which to enjoy the chutney – he only wanted to eat it all by itself! And that is what he would do in a few minutes when he returned to the privacy of his room. Sitting on the edge of his bed in perfect solitude, with no fear of interruption, he would revel in his shameful gluttony.

If he could wait that long.

Reaching up, he selected a jar right in the middle of the row, moving the rest together again to close the gap. He clutched the jar to his chest possessively, then carefully slid the cupboard door back into place.

'Good evening, Father Laurence.'

The cook's even voice from the sanctity of her wicker chair – its high back hiding her from view – broke the silence and nearly gave the priest a heart attack.

'Joseph, Mary and all the saints!' Laurence yelped, shock causing him to lose his grip on the chutney so that as his arm jerked, the jar flew high into the air in front of him. Then, galvanised, he sprang forward and caught it just before it reached the floor.

'Oh dear me, I've obviously surprised you, Father Laurence,' Mrs Haines said, her voice taking on a slightly sinister tone. She stood up and turned to face him. 'Can I help you with something?'

Now, the priest knew he must use all his acting powers to get himself out of this situation and he drew himself up to his full height, staring down at the cook and trying to stop his knees from shaking.

'I hope I haven't disturbed you, Mrs Haines,' he said, 'but I happened to be passing and I thought I heard a noise… here in the kitchen, so I decided I had better glance in to make sure there was no intruder.'

He knew he was babbling nonsense, and he knew he would never pull the wool over the cook's eyes – she was far too canny for that. But what else could he say? How else could he explain his presence? Especially as he had a jar of her chutney clutched to his heart. Swallowing hard, he waited for some divine assistance... but then, wait a minute – the room was quite dark, with barely any light at all. Perhaps she hadn't noticed anything and couldn't even see what he was holding. Her eyes had never been that good.

Mrs Haines pursed her lips. 'Well, I have been sitting here for the last forty minutes,' she said, 'and I can assure you that I've heard no noise at all, absolutely none, Father Laurence. No intruder has darkened my doorstep. So – obviously you must have been very mistaken.'

The cook was a short, very stout lady, never without a small pair of rimless glasses on the end of her nose, and had a somewhat fiery reputation. As she moved over to stare up at the priest, a very satisfying gleam of triumph shone from her shrewd blue eyes. Got him! Now just let him get himself out of this! She'd known what he'd been up to all these years. Of course she had! And it had usually been on Fridays. Now at last he had some explaining to do.

But then, something in his expression caught her unawares, and she stepped back.

Father Laurence suddenly looked so... so crestfallen... so defenceless... so ridiculously childish, reminding the cook of one of her own sons, the naughty one who they could never do anything with. The man standing in front of her, looking like a whipped dog, could have been her own boy. Her own silly, wayward boy.

She waited for a moment. 'Um... now let's see, would you like a strong paper bag to take that back with you, Father Laurence?' she asked patiently. 'If you drop it again, it will have more chance of survival, if it's in a bag.'

And the priest, knowing that the game was up, breathed a long sigh. For surely this was the moment to admit his sin.

'Well, thank you, Mrs Haines... for the offer of a bag,' he said.

'I must ask you to forgive me for… for daring to, um, help myself to one of your jars of chutney.' She interrupted, pulling the two stools from beneath the table so that they could both sit down opposite each other for a moment.

'You need only have asked, Father Laurence,' she said quietly, 'and I would happily have given you a jar of our chutney.' She looked him straight in the eye. 'But the bigger problem I have is that I am now very short of jars because this… practice… has been going on for some time, hasn't it? And you have failed to return even one of them.'

The priest's shoulders drooped miserably as he sat looking at his accuser. It had always seemed easier to wash out each stolen jar after he had scraped it clean with his spoon, and then dispose of it in the nearest town rubbish bin, rather than trying to return it without being seen. Avoiding detection had always been the name of the game. He found his voice at last.

'I can only deeply apologise for my behaviour, Mrs Haines,' he said humbly, trying to think of any line in one of Shakespeare's plays that might help him out. His mind flitted desperately through his repertoire… but then he had a brain wave!

'I am afraid that my only defence has to be that it's because of *you*… because of you and your expertise, Mrs Haines,' he said slowly. 'And your own, individual, truly *magnificent* way of producing food which is completely irresistible! Never before have I experienced such delights at table!' He paused for breath. 'Put quite simply Mrs Haines, I believe you were given a gift by God. And that is why I have been led astray.'

Looking across at her, something in her expression told him that he had won a point and he decided to push on. 'I must tell you something else, Mrs Haines,' he said. 'A long time ago, accepting that my sinful behaviour must top, I purchased a jar of green tomato chutney from the grocer's shop and was so terribly disappointed in it, I nearly spat it out! Really! It was quite disgusting, not a bit like yours! *You* could have shown them a

184

thing or two! And then, just to make sure, I tried another brand, a really famous brand, which had exactly the same effect!' He shook his head sadly. 'So you see, Mrs Haines, I am lost. I have been lost for a long time, as you already know, and it's all because of you. But I beg you to forgive me. To forgive me, Mrs Haines, so that I may go in peace. And sin no more,' he added, darting her a quick glance.

This was almost too much for Mrs Haines and she dabbed a hanky to her nose. 'There, there,' she said. 'Of course I forgive you, Father Laurence. None of us is perfect.' She looked across at him and smiled quite a sweet smile. 'But – would you be so kind as to provide me with a supply of new jars? You obviously know the ones I use – not that I shall need them just yet of course, because I shan't be making more chutney until the autumn. But, you know, next time you're in the market – the jars are cheapest in the market – a couple of dozen would be fine, to be going on with.'

'I shall let you have them without delay, Mrs Haines,' Laurence Dunn said.

She stood up and went over to the cupboard which had a deep drawer beneath it and from which she selected a small, strong, brown paper bag. Then she turned to the priest, who was standing awkwardly as he waited for the final screw of his humiliation to be turned.

'Let me have the chutney,' Mrs Haines purred, 'and I will put that heavy little jar safely inside this bag, Father Laurence. That's it. That's the way.'

They stood without speaking for a few moments, then he turned to go, pausing at the door.

'Thank you, Mrs Haines,' he said quietly. 'Thank you for…'

'Goodnight, Father Laurence,' the cook said. 'Sleep well.'

Chapter 23

Sitting at her dressing table, Elizabeth Mason leaned forward to examine her appearance more closely. She smiled a trifle ruefully. These days, there was no doubt that she was looking less and less like her beautiful daughter and more and more like her mother, who had died at the age of sixty.

Elizabeth carefully removed her diamante earrings and returned them to their rightful place among her other pairs, of which she had too many too count. But the ones she had worn tonight at dinner had always been her favourite, though they pinched unmercifully, which was why she had slipped upstairs for a few moments to take them off.

Her expression clouded as she thought about Honora, their one and only child. For several months Honora had not been her usual happy self. Something was wrong, Elizabeth was sure of it, although when she'd very lightly broached the subject, Honora had brushed off her mother's anxieties with a rather irritable – 'Oh, don't fuss, Mother. Of course I'm all right. Why shouldn't I be?'

And that was the question Elizabeth would like answered. Why shouldn't their daughter be content? She had been given everything in life that one could possibly want and had never been denied a single thing. Just listen to her now, playing those Chopin pieces on her beautiful white baby grand piano – her tenth birthday present – in the drawing room! She had always had the best music teachers, and had achieved a professional standard. Everyone said so, always so complimentary when they listened to her perform for them after one of the Mason's dinner parties. Not only that, she had had good private schooling, from an early age had been taken to countless concerts and theatre productions, and her spectacular birthday parties were the main topic of conversation for many days afterwards between those lucky enough to have been invited. To receive an invitation to one of Honora Mason's celebrations had been considered a great privilege, especially as each guest had always been presented with an expensive present to take home with them later.

Elizabeth heaved a sigh as her thoughts ran on. So why wasn't their daughter full of the joys of life as she should be? Because whatever Honora said to the contrary, for the last few months she had not been herself.

Elizabeth got up and went towards the door. She had better go back downstairs to rejoin Jacob and Honora or they would be wondering if she was all right. They had just enjoyed a wonderful dinner of roast Welsh lamb with all the trimmings, followed by their cook's very rich and creamy bread and butter pudding – of which, rather unwisely, Elizabeth had had two helpings. She had always had a somewhat unpredictable tummy.

As she went past the long picture window looking over the extensive garden, she stopped briefly to gaze out. It was a perfect summer evening – light and balmy – and the fragrance of the newly mown lawn was almost intoxicating as it reached her nostrils.

Elizabeth sighed again. Why couldn't everything in life be perfect like this? Why was there always something to fret about, to worry about?

Then suddenly realization hit her. Of course! She knew now!

Honora was being kept waiting too long for her wedding day. She and Alexander had been engaged for more than eighteen months – far too long when you thought about it – and the poor girl must be wondering what on earth was the matter because the actual date for the nuptials still hadn't been mentioned.

Elizabeth's mouth hardened. It was all very well for Alexander to have changed course in his ambitions, but hadn't he thought about how his fiancée might feel about that? To train to be a doctor was a very lengthy process, demanding endless time, endless study, leaving little room for personal relationships, which was probably why Alexander appeared to be holding back. But in Elizabeth's opinion that was extremely selfish. Every young woman dreamed of her own special day and, after all, Honora was almost 24. How much longer did he expect her to wait for him? No wonder the poor girl had been down in the mouth lately!

Elizabeth left her bedroom and went down the stairs, her mind made up. She was going to do something about this. It was time for Alexander Garfield to be given a little shove in the right direction so that wedding plans could start going ahead. Didn't he realise just what it took to arrange a big wedding – a big society wedding? The heir to Mason's Steel marrying the heir to the Garfield Tobacco empire – two immensely successful businesses of very long standing – would be of huge local, if not national, interest. Elizabeth Mason was going to make sure that no stone was left unturned. Over the past weeks and months she and Honora had looked in all the shops, perused all the glossy magazines showing wedding dresses, colour schemes, flower arrangements, venues for post ceremony banquets – the list was endless. All you needed was the money, and there would never be any shortage of that. Jacob Mason would see that his beloved daughter was the centre of attention at the wedding of the century. And his wife would certainly share the glory. Elizabeth had already chosen her own outfit – well, she had marked out two possibilities for her final decision, one to be worn if it was cold and one for a summer event.

She gritted her teeth. It was so aggravating not to know when it was going to be!

Downstairs, she went to open the drawing room door but paused for a moment to collect herself. All those thoughts about the reticence of her prospective son in law had made her quite hot and bothered. Then, taking a deep breath, she entered, smiling brightly.

'Oh, don't stop playing, Honora!' Elizabeth exclaimed, 'I was really enjoying those pieces, and you have such a lovely touch!'

But Honora took her hands from the keys, closed the lid of the piano, and went across to sit on the long sofa opposite her father. Jacob, fully replete after his dinner, was half asleep, but as Elizabeth came in, he roused himself, patting the seat beside him for her to sit down.

'Yes, very nice, Honora,' he said. 'I love all those songs.'

'They are not songs, Father,' Honora said. 'They are Chopin's famous nocturnes – music of the night for when the clamour of the day is done.' She smiled across. 'But I'm glad you like them.'

Elizabeth sat forward, clearing her throat. 'Honora – I really think we should have a chat about things. I mean, time is going on my dear, and we need to start making plans.'

There was a brief silence, then Honora said, 'You mean about the wedding?'

'Well, of course I mean the wedding!' Elizabeth exclaimed. 'Haven't you and Alexander been discussing it? After all, you've been engaged for well over a year – people will begin to think that there's something amiss!'

'Well – as a matter of fact there is something amiss,' Honora began, and Elizabeth almost exploded.

'I *knew* it!' she exclaimed. 'Alexander is so wrapped up in his own life, in his wretched career plans, that he has no time for anything or anyone else! Well, I'm not having it! He must make up his mind – you must insist on it, Honora!'

'Calm down, dear,' Jacob said anxiously. He hadn't seen his

wife het up like this for ages. 'I'm sure Honora and Alexander have been discussing everything together, and in due course we shall all be informed when the happy date is to be.' He patted his wife's knee. 'Everyone knows that weddings, and all that goes with them, are often the cause of family upset and arguments but don't let's go down that road before the journey has even begun, Elizabeth. It will all turn out as you wish it to, my dear. I'm sure of it.'

Honora decided that this was her moment. The moment she'd been dreading for months, and she straightened up.

'I rather doubt that things are going to turn out as you both wish,' she said slowly. 'In fact, I know they aren't. But I'm afraid my mind is made up and nothing is going to change it.'

'What… whatever are you talking about, Honora,' Elizabeth said. 'Please – what is it?'

'I have asked Alexander to release me from our engagement, and he has agreed,' Honora said simply. 'In fact, he fully understands my position, and has given me his blessing.'

The atmosphere in the room was electric at this information. Jacob seemed unable to utter a word, while Elizabeth had visibly blanched. Then she said faintly, 'Don't you love Alexander anymore, Honora? But why not? What has changed? You have always been everything to each other, you've been a pigeon pair almost from birth, haven't you?' Then Elizabeth's yes glinted angrily. 'But of course, I know what's changed your mind, Honora! You are fed up at playing second fiddle to Alexander's career prospects, and who can blame you! Good heavens, you hardly see anything of him these days! It was bad enough when he was away at college, but this medical ambition of his has put quite a different twist on things, hasn't it? He's engaged to his career, not to you, and I can understand why you—'

Elizabeth got no further before Honora rose from her seat and went over to kneel on the floor in front of her parents.

'No, Mother. You do not understand it, you do not understand anything,' she said quietly. 'I have been trying to find the courage to tell you all this, but you may as well hear it now.' Honora drew a deep breath. 'I have not stopped loving Alexander, and I will always love him with all my heart. But I realise now, that I do not want to be married to him, and maybe not to any man, ever,' she said. 'I want something much, much, more than being a wife and mother. I want to do something, anything, of some value.'

'So, is being a good wife and mother is not something of value?' Elizabeth's voice was cold. 'I have always done my best for you and your father, and I have been led to believe that my work with my charities has been fairly useful,' she added huffily.

'Of course, Mother,' Honora said. 'You are held in great respect in all you do, but… I am afraid the vision for my own future lies in another direction completely.'

'And what vision is that? Jacob said. 'What can you possibly want from life that we haven't already given you, Honora?'

Honora didn't hesitate. 'My freedom, Father, my freedom to be myself to make my own decisions. Because surely parents should not expect to own their children?' She leaned in towards them. 'I've decided that I want to train for a career, to get my teeth into something solid, something necessary and important to others, and I've been thinking that possibly I would like to follow a law career in some way.' She smiled. 'I have spent quite a few afternoons sitting in on cases at the law courts to observe exactly what goes on, how everything is done, and I found it fascinating, absolutely fascinating. And I thought that maybe with the right instruction, I could achieve at least something in that direction. I know it would take a long time and a lot of training, and I'd have to pass exams, but I'm in no hurry. I wouldn't mind waiting for years before actually getting a job, even a humble job,' Honora said.

'Getting a *job*?' Elizabeth said faintly. 'Why would any woman… a woman of any distinction… want a *job*? What's the attraction? You'll be telling us that you'd like to work in one of the factories next!'

'Working in a factory wouldn't bother me either,' Honora said calmly, 'but I have set my sights on something more intense, more demanding. I want to learn more about *life*.' She paused. 'I knew you wouldn't understand.'

Jacob decided to move the conversation slightly. 'You say that Alexander is happy about you breaking off the engagement? I'm sure he must be terribly upset. To be told that you no longer love him must have been extremely hurtful.'

'No, he isn't upset at all,' Honora said flatly. 'He saw my point of view straightaway.' She leaned back on her heels before going on slowly, 'We've had long discussions about all this, as you can imagine, and what neither of you understand is that although Alexander and I love each other dearly, and will always, always love each other, we've accepted that our true feelings are not those of a man and wife, but of brother and sister. Deep feelings, but not the feelings of lovers.'

'Well, why on earth did you get engaged?' Elizabeth demanded.

Honora shrugged. 'Because you expected it,' she said. From when we were quite small you – and Father – were always arranging for us to be together, treating us like twins, saying how well matched we were and of course we never argued it because we were so fond of each other. We were then, and nothing will change that. And when Alexander returned back safely after the war, the excitement and gratitude was overwhelming, and at the welcome home party it was you, Mother, who asked Alexander when he was going to pop the question.'

'I don't remember doing that,' Elizabeth said sulkily.

'Well, you did, but you had had rather a lot to drink,' Honora said. 'Besides, Alexander is so kind, he wouldn't have wanted to hurt my feelings so of course he did ask me whether I would like to be his wife at some point in the future. And then it was Christmas, everyone was so thrilled that the country was no longer at war – it was like being caught up in a whirlwind of colourful emotions.'

Jacob got up from the sofa and took hold of Honora's hands to raise her to her feet.

'I can't say that all this has come as welcome news, Honora,' he said, 'because – as you have already mentioned – your mother and I have always had the feeling that you and Alexander were meant to be together. But...' Jacob cleared his throat. 'We were clearly wrong, and all we want for you, my dear, is your happiness. If, as you say, you would like to try your hand at a career in the law, then you will go to the best college money can buy and we will see what happens after that.'

Honora put her arms around Jacob's neck. 'Thank you, Father,' she said simply. 'I want to make you proud of me, and I want to be proud of myself, to see what, if anything, I am actually capable of doing. I want to earn my own money, not keep spending yours.'

Elizabeth sat back utterly deflated. No wedding after all, no fusing of the Mason and Garfield families, despite all early expectations.

She sniffed. Never mind. She was still going to buy those two outfits she'd had her eye on, because there was sure to be some important future function or other when she could wear them.

She sighed heavily. It seemed that you could never be sure of anything with children.

Chapter 24

At eight o'clock on Monday as arranged, Alexander tapped on Angelina's sitting-room door and waited. It opened almost immediately, and she stood aside for him to enter. She didn't smile but looked up at him anxiously.

He spoke first, also unsmiling. 'Did you have a pleasant weekend – with your boyfriend?' he asked. 'The weather must have been perfect for walking in the country.'

She frowned briefly. Why were they talking about the weather when she was waiting to hear the important news he'd said he had for her?

'Yes, the weather was lovely,' she said, 'but what I want to know, Alexander, is what you had come to the hospital to tell me the other night. Your unexpected presence, and what you had to say – little though it was – left me feeling very disturbed. I thought something must be terribly wrong for you to take the trouble to seek me out as you did. And anyway, how did you know where I was – where I worked?'

'Oh, I've always known where you are, Angelina,' he said. 'Wherever possible, my father is keen to be kept informed about all his children, particularly those for whom he has good reason to be especially proud. That is certainly so in your case, and he has never stopped telling me about your successful career and aspirations.'

Angelina shrugged apologetically. 'Sorry about that,' she said lightly. 'But... do tell me what's wrong, Alexander. I'm desperate to know why you felt you needed to tell me something important – and why you made the effort to come to the hospital to do it. I'm surprised you were able to track me down.'

'That wasn't difficult,' he said, 'because I'm working there myself at the moment – as from last week.'

'*What?*' Angelina was mystified. '*You* are working at UCL? Why?'

'Because I am following in your footsteps, Angelina. I have switched my career to train as a doctor, and I've been on a team at Guy's until now, though a few of us are on secondment here at UCL – just for four weeks.' He smiled the disarming smile that always made Angelina's heart flutter. 'I've been expecting to bump into you,' he said, 'and of course, we trainees are all regular patrons of the canteen bar, which was the first place I thought of looking for you.'

Angelina sat down, finding it difficult to take in this unexpected news. But, annoyingly, she still didn't know what he'd had to tell her that night. She pulled out their other chair, and he sat down next to her, moving in quite close. Angelina stared across at him.

'And how is Honora?' she said calmly. 'Is she happy about what your new plans are? Does she see her future as being a busy doctor's wife?'

'Well, that is what I have come to talk to you about, Angelina,' Alexander said slowly. He waited before going on. 'The fact is, Honora has given me back her ring. We are no longer engaged to be married, and that situation will be permanent.'

For a few seconds, Angelina could do nothing but keep staring at him. This was the most unbelievable news... news she would not have expected in a million years.

'But – I don't understand,' she said slowly. 'You and Honora have always been so close, so… together… as a couple. What can have happened to make her change her mind?'

Alexander shrugged briefly. 'She has changed her mind about her whole life,' he said. 'She explained that she wishes for something more than being a wife and mother and has set her sights on – perhaps in the future – practising law.' He half-smiled. 'Honora is a very intelligent girl, and very determined. I hope she makes it. I really hope she achieves her goal.'

Angelina leaned forward towards him. 'I'm so sorry, Alexander,' she said quietly. 'It must have been very hurtful to be – to be – told that Honora does not love you anymore.'

'Oh, she hasn't said that,' Alexander said at once. Then, slowly, he went on, 'I know Honora loves me very much – as I love her – and nothing will change that. But we now both realise that our feelings are not those of a man and his prospective wife, but more as two long-term friends. Two best friends.' He smiled awkwardly. 'Our engagement was a rather rushed affair, I'm afraid, born out of, well, excitement and gratitude that I had survived the war. And I have to say, very much egged on by Honora's parents whose lifelong ambition has been that I should one day become their daughter's husband.' He sighed. 'I've got to confess, Angelina, that Honora's rejection came as a huge relief to me because I had been trying to find the right moment to do the same thing – to reject her. That is bizarre, isn't it? She came to my aid so that I didn't have to do the hurtful deed.'

'So – were your feelings exactly the same as Honora's?' Angelina said, mystified at this news. 'Had you realised that, after all, you were not ready for marriage because of your career hopes?'

'Not exactly,' Alexander said. 'The fact is, I love someone else.'

'Oh?' Angelina said. 'Have you known her long?'

'Yes, all my life,' he replied. 'And I think I've always realised that she is the woman I want to spend the rest of my days with – if only she'll have me.'

Then, in the silence that followed, he gently drew Angelina to her feet and looked deep into her eyes. 'Angelina – you *must* know that I am talking about you,' he said softly. 'It is you that I love.'

'Me?' Angelina whispered, unable to cloak her incredulity.

'Surely you remember France,' he said, 'and how I held you in my arms? And how you said you were sorry that we were kissing and I told you not to be sorry because I wasn't sorry at all. And I wasn't. For those treasured moments, I was in heaven! It was then that I finally realised that I had loved you for most of my life, not just because you are beautiful, but because you are clever and courageous. And you are kind, Angelina. You are a very, very special person.'

He waited before going on quietly. 'When I brought my men to that Clearing Station, it never crossed my mind that I would see you there. The line of battle was a very long one. But from the moment I set eyes on you, I was transfixed by the way you were treating every one of the wounded – I just stayed and watched you going from one stretcher to another, consoling and reassuring each of them while dealing calmly with their bleeding, open wounds, with their cries for help. I watched you hold their hands, and smile down at them. They must have thought you were a visiting angel, because that is exactly what you looked like, Angelina.'

He held her to him tightly. 'You are the most extraordinary woman I am ever likely to meet. It would be a privilege to be your husband – if you will have me.'

For a moment Angelina thought she might drop to the floor in a dead faint. This was her childhood dream come true! But had she really heard all those things, had he really said them?

Realising that he had taken her completely by surprise, Alexander said quietly, 'I understand why you are hesitating Angelina, because your career will always be important to you, and rightly so. I would never wish to stand in your way and I would happily wait for you until you are fully qualified. Until you are ready to trust me with the rest of your life – and your future. Our future together.'

It was fortunate that he was holding her to him because Angelina's knees were trembling. She dropped her head onto his shoulder, still finding it impossible to speak.

'But perhaps I am going too fast, and taking too much for granted,' Alexander went on. 'Because it was obvious that your boyfriend – Dennis? – is very proud to be with you. Do you love him as much as he clearly loves you, Angelina? Because if so, forget everything I've said, and I will move out of your life once and for all.'

Now she clutched Alexander to her, nestling her face into his neck, loving the feeling of his strong frame melding with her soft curves. 'How can you say such a thing, Alexander?' she said, her whispered words muffled. 'Of course, I do like Dennis very much. He's great fun to be with, but you must know that I have worshipped you for as long as I can remember. I have dreamed that, one day, you would ask me to marry you, but that was all it was – a pointless dream. Why would you want to marry me when you had Honora? And why would I, a hapless orphan, ever hope to become a member of your important family? My dream didn't make any sense, and it doesn't now, really. Because I find it impossible to believe.'

Now he bent his head, tilting her chin to reach his lips. He kissed her, softly at first, then with such intensity it almost took her breath away.

She would never know how long they remained there together as he kissed her over and over again, whispering in her ear that he would love her for the rest of his life. But eventually he released her gently and gazed down.

'Does that convince you, Angelina?' he said. 'Can I make you believe that we were meant to be together for ever?'

She pulled away, and gazed up into his eyes. 'Yes, Alexander,' she said softly. 'I really believe that my dream has come true at last.'

He could see her tears beginning to well, and he closed his lips over her eye lids. 'And does that mean that you agree to become my wife – at a point convenient to your career obligations?' He smiled down at her. 'I would never stand in your way, Angelina,' he said, 'because I am very well aware of how strong your ambitions have always been. It has already been proved that you have far too much to give to the world, and nothing should ever put a stop to that.'

She returned his smile, at last feeling herself begin to relax. 'I know that in its own time everything will come right for us, Alexander,' she said. 'I hope to finish my degree, and eventually to become a surgeon – an ambition I have had for a long time.' She snuggled into him again. 'But somewhere in the middle of all that, I want a lovely white wedding with the man I will always adore. And that's my promise, Alexander. To adore you for ever.'

He heaved a long sigh. What more could any man ask for? But Angelina hadn't quite finished.

'One advantage which all our children are going to have,' she said, 'is that they will be born into a loving family that would *never* abandon them and leave them to fate.' She smiled. 'Not only that,' she murmured, 'but, naturally, there are always going to be two doctors on hand to care for them and see them thrive.'

Chapter 25

December 1921

In his study, Randolph Garfield knelt down in front of the fire and picked up the poker to move the coals around a bit. They burned and crackled brightly, sending a warming glow into the room.

But Randolph didn't need a fire to warm his heart, because he had not felt this happy for many, many years.

He glanced at the clock. Jacob would be here any minute for their usual get-together, and Randolph had selected a special bottle of red to go with the cold roast beef and sliced tongue they would be enjoying for their supper.

At eight o'clock Jacob Mason arrived, and soon the two men were sitting opposite each other. As usual, Jacob asked the perennial question.

'So, Randolph,' he enquired, 'how is business? Good, I hope!'

Randolph nodded briefly. 'Yes, thank you, Jacob. Despite the aftermath of the war and the ensuing pandemic, we have somehow come through – relatively unscathed. And you, Jacob? I did hear that you were having some staffing problems at Mason Steel.'

Jacob brushed that aside. 'Oh – nothing too serious,' he said, 'but of course quite a few of our men did not return from battle… and some of them were our best workers as it happens. Which was a nuisance.'

'I'm sure it was more of a nuisance to them – and to their families – that they did not return,' Randolph said tartly.

Aware of the rebuke, Jacob said, 'Yes, yes of course. I did manage to track down some of them afterwards, and leave the back pay which their sons would have received… had they returned.'

He cleared his throat, deciding to change the subject. 'And what of the Garfield, Randolph? I hear that it is still a highly successful and very happy enterprise. So I imagine you are not thinking of selling it, or passing it on to others – if someone would take it off your hands! An orphanage is never going to be an investment, and there can have been nothing in it for you apart from personal satisfaction.'

For a few seconds, Randolph found it hard to reply. He was not going to try and convince his friend – the friend he could cheerfully throttle at times – just what had been 'in it' for him, Randolph Garfield. No amount of money on earth could give him the satisfaction, the pure pleasure he had received over the years. When he had picked up that newborn baby off the street, it had changed his life. And as it was turning out, would go on doing so for ever

'The Garfield Home for Children will remain just that for as long as it is possible to forecast,' Randolph said quietly. He glanced at his friend. 'And it will go on producing children of whom we can be proud – even though their provenance is rarely known.'

Jacob realised he had touched a nerve, and broke in quickly. 'Yes, I accept that, in general terms,' he said, 'because in fact my foreman has suggested we accept two more of your orphans who are due to leave the orphanage at the beginning of the year. They are brothers of a young man already employed in the factory and the foreman thinks we can do ourselves nothing but good by taking the younger boys on. He is of the hopeful opinion that they might be of the same calibre… honest, hard-working and resourceful. And I have agreed to give them a trial.' Jacob smiled expansively. 'Time will tell so we'll just wait and see,' he added.

'Indeed, you are right, Jacob,' Randolph said, 'and as you have remarked on more than one occasion, it is all in the genes. I am sure you will have no reason to doubt your foreman's opinion.'

'Well, I hope not,' Jacob replied stoutly.

Presently, tucking into his cold meat and freshly baked bread, Jacob glanced over at Randolph.

'I feel that we – Elizabeth and I – owe you an apology, Randolph,' he said.

'Really, Jacob?' Randolph reached for his glass of wine and sipped. 'Do go on.'

'Well, it's about our wayward daughter, Randolph! We cannot understand, either of us, what has got into her in wanting to qualify at something and earn her own money! Why on earth does she feel the need to do that? She has always been given everything she's ever wanted – you know that, Randolph.' Jacob gave a sidelong glance. 'And you must feel very disappointed that she has given Alexander back his ring, and that they are no longer engaged. Not just disappointed, Randolph, but you must be upset and angry that your son has been rejected! That cannot be a comfortable thought for you – as any parent would understand.'

Randolph tried – and almost failed – to hide a smile. 'Oh, well – Jacob, please don't concern yourself. My son is a fully grown adult and he went through a lot – as did many others – during the war. I am sure that has helped him to face up to whatever fate throws at him. And I am also sure that he and Honora will remain firm friends for the rest of their lives,' Randolph added.

Jacob looked away. This was the first time that any discussion about the broken engagement had taken place, because it had all been kept quiet until the dust had settled. Until they'd hoped Honora would come to her senses. But now that it was obvious that her mind was fully made up, it was best to clear the air.

'To be honest, Randolph, I believe the wretched Suffrage movement is to blame for all this,' Jacob said. 'Giving women the vote has put ridiculous ideas into their heads! What will they want next? Equal pay, equal rights? But women are not equal, Randolph, and never will be! They are the weaker, fairer sex, they do not have the same physical strength or brain power as us men – and their place is in the home to care for their husbands and children!' No good will come of this emancipation, Randolph! You mark my words!'

Presently, when supper was over, Jacob stood up to take his leave. 'So, Randolph…' he said. 'You're sure that there are no hard feelings about our daughter's behaviour… her decision? Elizabeth and I would hate for any bad feelings to exist between us. Not after all these years.'

Randolph patted Jacob's shoulder. 'You may rest assured about that, Jacob,' he said kindly. 'And I have the feeling that our youngsters know exactly what they're doing, and that everything will turn out for the best. You just wait and see.'

After Jacob had gone, Randolph returned to the study, poured the last of the wine into his glass and finished it. He smiled. That was a little toast to himself and to his own future happiness – which he had never been more sure of.

Because earlier that month, Alexander had confided in him that Angelina Green had agreed to one day become his wife. It would not be yet, not until after the bride had qualified as a doctor, and they had decided to keep their promise to each other private until Christmas.

'Which will give me time to change my mind,' Angelina had teased.

But they had both known that that would never happen. After all, from the age of 7 she had dreamed that one day she would be Alexander's wife, and that dream was going to come true.

Nothing, and no one, could stop them now.

Epilogue

At the age of 26, Dr Angelina Green became Dr Alexander Garfield's wife. She continued her mission to become an orthopaedic surgeon, and she achieved this, her training briefly interrupted by giving birth to their three children – two boys and a girl.

Long before that, and with Angelina walking behind her to the altar, Ruby Lane married Robert Walker. The hairdressing salon continued to be so successful that another, larger, one was opened in the area – run almost entirely by Ruby, who also had to satisfy the demands of clients who insisted that she alone should do their hair. She gave birth to two daughters, to the special delight of Grandma Walker who'd always longed for a little girl in her family.

Honora Mason went on to pass her exams in the legal system and found a position in a busy solicitor's office in London. She never married.

Emma Kingston remained as superintendent of the orphanage until well into her eighties, afterwards her wise counsel being regularly sought by her successor.

Mrs Marshall made a partial recovery from her illness, and after the sudden death of her brother worked at the orphanage on a part-time basis, helping Mrs Haines in the kitchen.

Maria Jones eventually left the orphanage to become full-time nanny to Angelina's children. She would live with the Garfield family for the rest of her life.

Laurence Dunn continued at the priory until his retirement, after which he became a volunteer at the Globe, showing theatre-goers to their seats and helping to clear up their mess afterwards. For this he was given a free seat for every performance. Of course, Mrs Haines forgave him, even though she'd known what the blighter had been up to all along.

Despite being in his seventies, Randolph Garfield remained as head of Garfield Tobacco, still preferring to walk the familiar route home each evening, past the docks and human detritus towards the orphanage. His grandsons would one day take up the helm at Garfield Tobacco.

Did you love *Front Line Nurse*? Don't miss *Lexi's War*, another unputdownable novel from Rosie James. Available now!

Dear Reader,

Thank you so much for taking the time to read this book – we hope you enjoyed it! If you did, we'd be so appreciative if you left a review.

Here at HQ Digital we are dedicated to publishing fiction that will keep you turning the pages into the early hours. We publish a variety of genres, from heartwarming romance, to thrilling crime and sweeping historical fiction.

To find out more about our books, enter competitions and discover exclusive content, please join our community of readers by following us at:

🐦 *@HQDigitalUK*

f facebook.com/HQDigitalUK

Are you a budding writer? We're also looking for authors to join the HQ Digital family! Please submit your manuscript to:

HQDigital@harpercollins.co.uk.

Hope to hear from you soon!